Legacy of Love

Port Provident: Home to Love

Kristen Ethridge

Chapter One

WHITTEN PEOPLES STOOD on the raised wall that protected Provident Island from the ravages of nature's storms. Almost as soon as the scent of the coastal air hit his lungs, it didn't take long for Whitt to remember why he'd left town and had once vowed never to return.

Regret. It smelled like saltwater.

Unfortunately, it looked like Kaye Vontegarten. The phone call came through this morning and informed Whitt that his grandmother wasn't expected to make it through the night. He called his assistant and instructed her on what to book for his trip, then he packed a bag. When his plane from New York City landed at Bush Intercontinental Airport in Houston, he rented a car for the drive south to the coast and Port Provident, Texas.

Whitt stuck his hands in his pockets, balling his fists and pressing against the seam beneath his knuckles. He struggled to move the crisp, yet-still-humid air past the lump in his throat. Granny couldn't be going. She was the only link he had to his mother. And now she—and the love and memories she'd so generously shared with him his whole life—would be gone, just as gone as his mother was.

This would be the worst Christmas ever. You were supposed to get presents at Christmas, not lose them. Granny had been the greatest gift in his life. And before the needles would fall off the trees in homes all over Port Provident...Granny would leave this world for the next.

"Did you know this was where the Port Provident Children's Home stood before the Great Storm of 1910?"

Whitt turned his head as a woman spoke softly next to him. Her voice rose just barely over the sound of the perpetual motion of the waves below.

"No, I didn't."

"Right there, across the street."

He knew he should have been friendlier. He should have had some kind of reply for her wistful commentary. But not today. Not while his grandmother lay confined in a regulation-style hospital bed a few blocks away. Whitt spent his life immersed in technology. He spent his days coaching the next round of tech entrepreneurs—he helped save fledgling businesses with good ideas. But none of it could save Granny.

It made his heart hurt.

In a way, that surprised him more than anything else that had happened today, because Whitt Peoples was almost sure he didn't have a heart anymore.

"Do you live here?" The quiet voice asked another question.

"No, just visiting."

She pulled out a slick, colorful piece of paper, carefully folded into a narrow rectangle. "I'm Samantha Spaeth with the Port Provident Historical Society. We're dedicating a new exhibit at our Port Provident Historical Museum to the Children's Home and the heroism the night of the Great Storm of 1910."

Whitt took the folded paper and stuffed it in his pocket without more than a passing glance. "Y'all sure talk about the Great Storm a lot around here, don't you?" Whitt had spent the first ten years of his life on Provident Island. Then he moved to the city that never sleeps. From all appearances, Port Provident was still taking a nap, still stuck in the past.

"Hurricanes are a way of life here on the coast, Mr..."

Whitt could hear the question in her voice as the end of her sentence trailed off. Maybe if he answered her and played along for a moment, she'd leave him alone with the rest of his thoughts. A hundred meaningless dinner parties in New York's dining rooms and hotels had prepared him for moments like this.

"Peoples. Whitt Peoples. Nice to meet you, Ms. Spaeth."

It wasn't, but he'd do or say just about anything right now in order to be left alone for the few minutes he needed to compose himself before he went to Granny's bedside.

"Peoples? Are you related to Diana Peoples, by chance?"

Whitt nodded shortly. He'd intended to play a game, but not Twenty Questions.

"My grandmother."

A smile like a Gulf of Mexico sunrise spread across Samantha Spaeth's island-tanned face. "But you said you were just visiting."

"I am. I live in New York City now."

The glow continued to warm her features. "Well, you should come tomorrow, Mr. Peoples. We're honoring John Peoples as part of the exhibit."

A seagull squawked loudly from a weathered post that had been stuck out a dozen feet beyond the shoreline. Whitt knew precisely how the bird felt. He wanted to squawk and flap this woman away. "Who?"

"John Peoples, your great-grandfather!"

She practically squealed. Whitt sharply eyed the seagull on the post, trying telepathically to convince him to fly over here. Maybe he could flap his wings and scare the historical cheerleader off.

"Never knew him." Whitt looked at his watch. Ten more minutes until he had planned to check in on the one grandmother who still mattered to him.

"Of course not. He died several decades ago." She held out another brochure and pointed at a photo on the front. "But Diana and some other members of your family will be there. It would be an honor to have you there with them."

He could respond to her enthusiasm truthfully—and look like a total loser. But not only did he not have any idea who John Peoples was, he didn't know Diana well. Nor did he really know any of the other members of the Peoples family still here in Port Provident.

And—he didn't really care to. It wasn't like they'd followed up with him after he and his dad moved away from Port Provident when Whitt was ten. They hadn't cared about having him in their life. Why should he care about being in theirs?

The only person he cared about on Provident Island was dying in ICU. He wasn't about to waste time shaking hands and giving air kisses to people he hadn't seen in more than twenty years.

Honesty was the best policy.

If Whitt told her why he was really here, she'd feel sorry for him and leave him alone. That's what strangers did. They went away when things got uncomfortable.

Well, strangers and most members of the Peoples family.

"I'm afraid I'm only here for a few days. I've come because of a death in the family. In fact, I need to take care of a few things."

"Oh, I'm so sorry."

"It's okay." Another lie, but he didn't care. He'd save truth—all of it—for his grandmother. That's what final goodbyes were for.

And on that note, it was time to say goodbye to the blonde stranger next to him. At another time, in another place, he might have bought her a drink, might have asked her some stupid pick-up-line questions. But not now. Not today.

He felt the brochure bend between his fingers and noticed there was a trash can up ahead. If he could get far enough down the sidewalk on Gulfview Boulevard, it would make the chances of her seeing him dumping her invitation to the museum-based Peoples family reunion very slim. Whitt had absolutely no intentions of attending tomorrow's highlight of the Port Provident holiday social season, but he also didn't want to hurt the poor woman's feelings. After all, he figured she wouldn't be outside on a sidewalk above the Gulf of Mexico in the week before Christmas handing brochures to passers-by if she didn't care deeply about her job and the event.

Granny had always reminded him to think about the impacts of his actions on others—even the small gestures. It had been good advice.

He couldn't keep his thoughts off Granny and the life lessons she'd always tried to instill in him. The knowledge that most likely, after tonight, there'd be no more soft-spoken wisdom from her lips and her heart...well, the harsh thought leveled on him like a weight the size of Texas.

A gust of December sea breeze blew in as Whitt picked up his small bag and walked down the sidewalk at the edge of the Gulf. Having lived in New York for twenty years, Whitt never would have believed a winter breeze on a Texas island could chill him to the bone.

But at this moment, he felt colder than he ever had in his life.

He knew it wasn't the wind.

SAMANTHA DROPPED THE last stack of brochures on the counter at Café Provident, the island's favorite coffee shop. Located in the heart of Port Provident's historic downtown shopping area, the artistic café was popular with locals and received plenty of foot traffic from tourists out shopping for the holidays. Samantha needed to finish her mission strong by grabbing as much attention of both groups as she could in the next twenty-four hours.

One of the museum's board members had pulled a few strings and secured national journalist Reid Knight to come and report on the museum and the Great Storm for his new show, America's Small Town Surprises. The show was about to launch on HSH, the Home Sweet Home network and the first episode would feature Port Provident. Samantha knew it was critical that they have a good turnout and showcase the city, as well as Port Provident's unique history.

"Hey this looks promising," Samantha said as she arranged the slick paper next to the cash register. "All the brochures I put out last week are gone. Has anyone said anything about coming? Any chit-chat while people are waiting at the counter?"

Beth Greenling, the owner of Café Provident, finished a transaction at the register and handed a receipt to a customer with a smile, then turned toward Samantha.

"A few have. Becca from the animal shelter was in here over the weekend, and she said has it on the calendar."

Samantha smiled. "I wonder what happened to all the animals that night. I can't even imagine the chaos. People had to be just sick about making choices about keeping themselves and their children alive. I wouldn't think there would be much time to help the pets too. So sad."

Beth nodded. "I think I would have been terrified. I'm glad the Gulf was quiet this past summer. I read a report that they're predicting a more active season next year—I really hope that doesn't come to pass. But I'm always fascinated by the stories that come out of disasters—you get to see that there are heroes around every corner."

"Which is exactly the point of this new exhibit. Without John Peoples' leadership, Port Provident likely wouldn't have been rebuilt. And without his heroism the night of the storm, well, Isabel Schuster and Ingrid Buchholz wouldn't have been saved, and there would have been no one to tell the story of the Children's Home—there would have been no connection to remember those innocent lives."

Beth stirred a splash of milk into Samantha's coffee. "You know, I moved here to get away from corporate America, to leave the rat race behind. I wanted to disconnect and look at the beach every day—you know, enjoy the solitude and doing my own thing. But I think I'm more connected than ever. I love this community. I love the people of Port Provident and the history that's happened here over the years and how it still shapes and defines this city, even today."

"Oh, me too." Samantha inhaled the scent of the warm, roasted beans that filled Café Provident. "When I had the chance to come work here, I hadn't grown up that far away, so I knew about the Great Storm, but I didn't know much else. I mainly came for the beach."

Samantha took a cautious sip of the hot coffee Beth had handed her. "But during the last few years, I've learned so much about this place. I haven't just learned the history, I've gotten involved at First Provident Church, and I've made some true friends—which, in turn, means I've learned a lot about myself. You know, working on this Children's Home project has been freeing. It's like there are no secrets anymore about this huge part of the city's history. I like that—we're unearthing the surprises of history at the center. I'm the girl who never even wanted surprise parties as a kid."

"No surprise parties? Oh, boo. Where's the fun in that, Sam?" Beth handed her friend two bills and some coins in change.

"Order. Detail. Being prepared. It's a great feeling. Now, I need to get enough people to come so we make a splash on that TV show. I've got all my fingers crossed—I've just gotta keep hustling for the next few hours."

"Pfft."

Samantha heard a forceful hiss from the doorway of the café.

"Crossing fingers will only get you a hand cramp. I wish someone could explain the point of walking around with twisted fingers. Don't people pray anymore?"

The bell overhead jingled as Diana Peoples, town matriarch and benefactor of the Port Provident Historical Society, walked through Café Provident's door.

"Ha. I knew you'd say that, Diana." Samantha smiled. During the past year as she'd worked on this exhibit, Diana had become a friend and mentor—almost like a grandmother. She was full of advice and wisdom and knew more about the people and history of Port Provident than nearly anyone else Samantha had met on Provident Island.

The thought of people she'd met triggered an idea in Sam's mind. "I met someone today who said he knows you."

Diana brightened the winter day with the warmth of her smile. "Well, that's the bonus of living your whole life in one place...you get to know lots of people. Who was it?"

"Whitten Peoples. He said he was your grandson, and he was just in town for a few days because of a death in the family. So, he couldn't make it to the event tomorrow. If something's going on and you can't make it either, just let me know."

Diana took a slight step backward. If Samantha hadn't been making eye contact as they spoke, she never would have noticed.

The color fell from Diana's cheeks like the unusual snowfall the island had seen last Christmas.

"Whitt is here?"

Samantha nodded. "That's what he said his name was. He was about six-foot-two and had dark brown hair and dark brown eyes. Sound about right?"

The older woman nodded briefly and made a general noise of agreement. "*Mmhmm*. I...um, I guess so, yes."

The end of Diana's sentence came out strong, but Samantha had noticed her initial struggle for words. Something wasn't adding up.

"Beth, can I get my latte to go?"

Diana was a regular at Café Provident, and Beth knew what her regulars liked. She'd started preparing her order as soon as Diana walked through the door.

"Of course, Diana. Here." Beth pushed a white lid tightly around the rim of the cup and handed it to Diana. "It'll be four-seventy-nine."

Diana held the cup in one hand and dug in her designer brown leather purse. Her movements were jerky. "Here you go. Keep the change, dear."

She leaned forward and put a twenty-dollar bill on the counter and then turned and walked out the door without saying another word.

"Well, that's a first," Beth said as she counted out the change and dropped it into the tip jar. The coins made a loud clink as they came to rest on the rest of the day's gratuities. "I have never seen Diana Peoples just leave. She always says goodbye. Do you think everything's okay?"

"I don't know." Samantha looked out the window and watched Diana's car until it turned at the end of the block. "It was like she saw a ghost."

WHITT STOOD OUTSIDE the door to Granny's assigned room at Provident Medical Center. The steady beeps from the machines did nothing to steady his anxiety about what was going on within the tiny quarters.

"Mr. Peoples?" An older man in a white coat stopped alongside Whitt. "I'm Dr. Carlson. The nurses told me you were here. They'll have some paperwork for you to go over in a bit, but first, let me update you on Mrs. Vontegarten's condition."

Dr. Carlson spoke in clinical terms, giving Whitt a summary of his grandmother's condition. Whitt heard none of it. Instead, he watched the nurse swap out the IV bag that attached to the tubing in the frail hand. She made a few small adjustments, then peeled off the tape that held the IV in place. Patting Granny's hand gently, the nurse said something to her, then affixed another strip of tape to hold the tubing in place.

"Jeannie's a good nurse. She takes good care of her patients. Mrs. Vontegarten doesn't know what she's saying, but Jeannie treats everyone the same."

Whitt turned away from the scene in the room. "What do you mean Granny doesn't understand the nurse?"

"Well, she may technically be able to hear Jeannie, but your grandmother's been unresponsive for the last thirty-six hours or so. It's perfectly normal at this stage."

Whitt felt his heart break, like a fall leaf crushed in the palm of a child's hand. He noticed the pop and crackle as the curves flattened, as though nothing would ever be the same again.

Another nurse tapped Dr. Carlson on the shoulder and showed him a piece of paper. "I'll be back to check on her later this evening, Mr. Peoples."

Whitt nodded. It was all he could do.

He stood there, feet rooted to the heavy-duty vinyl tiles of the hospital hallway. He watched Jeannie adjust Granny's pillows and remembered crawling into a big four-poster bed the night his mother died.

Whitt rolled from his side to his stomach, unable to stop the tears. He pressed his face hard into the pillow. He smelled dust and feathers and the faintest hint of floral-scented laundry detergent.

He wanted to be with her, to go with her.

He was eight, and his world had just ended, washed away on a flood of tears.

Today in school, he'd presented his report on what he wanted to be when he grew up. Now, none of it mattered. He didn't want to grow up in a world without Mommy.

A gentle hand rubbed his back in a circle, smoothing the cotton of his T-shirt.

Sssh, she said, over and over. Sssh.

"I want to go with her too." She laid down beside him and wrapped him in her arms. "She's with the angels now. We'll see her again, Whitt. We'll see her again. But for now, we need to rest. We need to rest, and while we do, she'll still be with us in our dreams."

Jeannie crooked her finger and indicated for Whitt to come inside the room.

It broke the train of his memories, but soon all memories would be what Whitt had left.

He sighed. It hurt.

"She's resting comfortably, Mr. Peoples."

Whitt nodded. "I saw you taking good care of her. Thank you."

"Oh, Miss Kaye and I are old friends. I can't let her down." She beamed, then looked down at the bed-ridden woman and gave her hand a light squeeze.

"You know Granny?"

"Oh sure. I sing in the choir at First Provident. Even after she stopped being able to drive, Miss Kaye always made sure someone picked her up and brought her to church. She'd never miss a Sunday."

Whitt looked down at the thin frame under the white hospital sheet. Granny had changed so much since the last time he'd seen her.

Apparently, she'd changed in more ways than one.

"I only heard her talk about angels once in my life. I didn't know she went to church."

"She did. And we all loved her." The smile never left Jeannie's face. "I've got paperwork for you to sign, Mr. Peoples. She signed a Do Not Resuscitate order when she came in and gave us a Durable Power of Attorney with your name on it. I think she wanted to make things as easy on you as possible."

He watched the rise and fall of her chest, in time with the machines. "What does that mean?"

"It means that you're authorized to make healthcare decisions on her behalf, but that she does not want extraordinary measures taken to prolong her life. So, if she goes into cardiac arrest, I won't be getting a crash cart. She wants us to let her go."

"Go." The word popped out of Whitt's mouth, like the nurse was speaking a foreign language. The syllable felt dry and unfamiliar. "She wants to go."

"She hasn't been communicative for about three days, but when she was still in and out, she said she missed Julie."

He felt the saltwater of tears shed long ago prick at his eyes again. He breathed out and touched Granny's right hand. "I do, too."

Jeannie said nothing further, just patted him lightly on the shoulder as she passed.

Whitt felt the vellum-thin skin covering the back of Kaye's hand. The time between beeps seemed to linger. The nurse had said Granny tried to make this as easy as possible, but nothing would make this transition easy on Whitt.

His mother was gone. He hadn't really spoken to his father in years, except for surface conversations. They mostly communicated in short, periodic text messages. Even a random blonde stranger on Gulfview Boulevard knew more about his family than he did.

When the beeps stopped announcing the slowing march of Kaye Vontegarten's vital signs, when there was only silence to surround him instead of his granny's tight embrace...Whitt would be alone.

He'd spent his whole life pretending like flying solo was okay. He'd always been one to act tough and independent.

But deep down inside, where his heart tried to match the ebbing rhythm of the one in front of him, he knew it wasn't.

Chapter Two

"THE NURSES TOLD ME I'd find you in here." A quiet voice spoke from the direction of the door, breaking the general stillness that had surrounded Whitt and Granny. He didn't know who would be looking for him.

Whitt turned slightly in the chair and saw an older woman standing in the doorway.

She was a stranger, yet, completely familiar.

She had his dad's thin nose and strong chin. The gentle curve of her eyebrows and the faint rosiness of her cheekbones saved her features from having the same aloof look Steve Peoples had worn every day of his life.

He was pretty sure he knew who she was. But it had been a long time.

More than twenty years, to be specific.

"Do I know you?" The pit of his stomach had gone as cold as the snow blanketing the sidewalks in front of the building where he lived in New York. He'd been foolish to think he could come back to Port Provident quietly.

One grandmother didn't even know he was sitting there next to her, but yet, four hours hadn't even passed before the other one located him on her radar.

"It's been a while." She straightened her spine slightly and cleared her throat. "Diana Peoples. Your grandmother."

He nodded. As the head of a company that had many clients notable for perhaps being the "next big thing," Whitt felt comfortable giving interviews. He was media-trained and good with talking points.

But yet, he'd never wished for Anya Stein, his head of public relations, to be with him any more than in this moment. He'd do just about anything for a pre-written soundbite right about now.

"You came to see Granny?"

He knew once upon a time, Diana Peoples had attended church at First Provident every Sunday. Jeannie, the nurse, revealed earlier that Granny had as well. Maybe they ran into each other there. Maybe this was some reverse welcome committee thing.

Maybe Diana was the goodbye committee.

"I came to see you. Kaye and I buried all hatchets between us long ago. I told her goodbye while she could still hear it and accept my apologies."

"Your apologies?"

Diana's gray bob swayed gently with the movement of her head. "For not stopping your father twenty years ago. For keeping my mouth shut."

"For keeping your mouth shut?" Whitt didn't understand what she was getting at. Maybe Diana needed some of the good stuff they kept on lockdown here at Provident Medical Center.

"I tried so hard to keep the peace with my family."

"I'm sure Jake and Jenna appreciated it," Whitt said, naming off his two cousins, the children of his Uncle Johnny. Jake and Whitt had been inseparable in their younger years. They built sandcastles on the beach, tried—and failed—to surf, and generally excelled at causing the type of mischief that characterized the childhoods of most young boys.

Whitt had wondered about Jake many times during the years, but he'd always pushed the curiosities of his mind back in their tightly locked box. His father had always made it clear there would be no return to Port Provident. He'd always made it clear that they would never see the Peoples family again.

Only Granny had been his link back to the island where he'd been born and the mother who'd given him life.

"No, they didn't. The family and others in Port Provident asked about you for years. And I had to tell them the same thing every time. 'I'm sure they love living in the big city,' I'd say, with a high-watt smile stuck to my face. After a while, they stopped asking as much. Maybe they believed me. Maybe they finally forgot—just like Steve asked us all to do."

Whitt snapped out of the haze he'd been viewing this whole day through. But even though everything seemed clear for a brief moment, he didn't know what to say.

Steve Peoples had wanted to forget his life on the Texas coast, and he'd wanted those he'd left behind to do the same.

It seemed like mission accomplished. Well, for everyone but one person.

"How do you just forget someone?" Whitt asked quietly, barely louder than the steady cadence of electronic beeps.

"You don't."

The simple answer filled the room, pushing out all the half-finished thoughts in Whitt's mind. The truth of this moment was that from time to time during his life, he had wondered what he'd do if he encountered any of the people left behind in his former island home.

He used to wonder what would he do?

What would he say?

Now, that moment was undeniably here. And just as clear to him was the reality that the answer to those questions was frustratingly simple.

Nothing.

The answer was nothing.

He'd always planned on having the perfect turn of phrase, the perfect comeback, the perfect cutdown. For the people who never wrote, never called, never cared—he'd always known he'd demonstrate with total clarity that he hadn't needed them. He'd been just fine without them.

The silence settled. Each tick of the second hand on the wall made it harder for Whitt to say all the things he hadn't been able to put into words through the lonely years.

Diana took her gaze downward and looked in her purse as she dug inside. She pulled something out, but Whitt couldn't tell what it was. It stayed completely hidden, tucked tightly in the palm of her hand. She took three steps forward, coming across the room—then she stopped short in front of the high hospital-issue table over the foot of the patient's bed.

She pressed her hand deliberately on the tabletop, leaving behind a key.

Whitt heard a sharp intake of breath and watched as her shoulders pushed back, squaring off into a perfect T that ran perpendicular to her spine.

"I know Kaye's health had been declining. I heard she took a quick turn for the worse. I'm sure you just caught the first plane here. If you haven't had a chance to book a hotel room, that's the key to the garage apartment at my house. Jake lived there for a time after he returned to town, but he and his wife, Gracie, moved out recently. Their little girl is old enough now to need a bit more space for toys and things. Plus, there's another baby on the way. You're welcome to stay there as long as you'd like. I won't be up in your business. I only want you to know you always have a place in Port Provident."

The green digital light from one of the monitors caught the brass-colored shaft of the metal. Whitt stared down at the key to his grandmother's garage apartment, remembering playing there as a child. Once, he and Jake had read a book in school on pirates. The seafaring rogues had staked their claim to a secluded part of Provident Island more than two hundred years ago. For months after discovering that fact, he and Jake pretended to be pirates. Every day after school, they ran to their secret pirate hideout above Nana's garage.

Nana.

Jake hadn't thought of Diana as Nana in two decades.

Lost in swashbuckling memories from the past, Whitt didn't see Diana leave the room. He heard the click of the door and saw her shadow pass in the hallway.

Whitt leaned forward and brushed the key off the table and into his hand. In the avalanche of rushed travel, he'd asked his assistant to book a room at the Grand Provident for him. He wouldn't need the key, but it didn't seem right to leave it behind in the hospital room, either. He'd have his assistant mail it back to Diana once he returned home.

Settling himself as comfortably as he could in the hospital-issue chair next to the bed, Whitt forced himself to be content with listening to Granny's shallow breathing, at least for the moment.

As the minutes ticked by, Whitt closed his eyes, and for a moment saw the sun shining once again on the pirate hideout that had been the stuff of his childhood dreams. He'd still had the memories long after he got used to the sound of horns and bustle in the city—long after he'd forgotten the squawk of seagulls and the gentle roar of the waves.

He'd forgotten so much.

But now he remembered. He remembered, and it tore at his heart in cuts and slices.

SAMANTHA HAD JUST FINISHED hanging the last of the decorations for tomorrow's event, when all of a sudden, she heard her stomach let out a loud growl. Her hands flew down and clutched her midsection as she shiftily turned her head quickly from side to side, hoping no one heard her inadvertent tummy symphony.

Clearly, it was time to get dinner. She looked up at the clock.

Oh my gosh, it's far past time to get dinner.

Samantha knew she needed to hurry, or the only options available would come from a fast-food drive-through window.

And on a night when her mind was racing with thoughts about the day to come and all the questions she had for herself about whether or not had she done enough and would they have a good showing on the TV program—well, the only thing that sounded good for dinner at this moment was home cooking. In Port Provident, that meant only one place: the Down-Home Café.

Thankfully, it didn't take long to get across town when it wasn't tourist season. Within a matter of minutes, Samantha slid into a red vinyl booth tucked toward the back corner. The waitress placed a menu on the faded white Formica table in front of Samantha.

"Oh hi, Honey. You're the one who likes two lemons in her iced tea, aren't you?"

Samantha smiled and nodded. "Guilty as charged."

"I'll give you a sec to look at the menu, and I'll be back with that glass of tea—and those lemons." The waitress tapped the table, then turned and walked back toward the kitchen.

Samantha didn't even need to study the menu. She knew exactly what she wanted. A stressful situation like her current one called for nothing but the best comfort food of all time—fried chicken and mashed potatoes. In fact, tonight called for the extreme.

Tonight called for mashed potatoes with gravy—lots and lots of rich, thick white gravy.

While she waited for the waitress, Samantha idly looked at the old TV mounted on the far opposite wall. Some newscaster was droning on and on about the week's lackluster stock market results.

She quickly decided that subject was too depressing for her to pay any further attention to the broadcast. Samantha didn't want to think about poor monetary results. When people felt their wallets tightening up, they were less likely to give to charities like the Port Provident Historical Society. And these days, the society was pulling out all the stops to bring in donations to their own very dry bank accounts. And the next goal on that plan was the launch of the Great Storm exhibit and the publicity that being featured on Reid Knight's new show would hopefully bring.

Samantha pulled her eyes away from the television. As she scanned towards the front door of the Down-Home Café, she saw a face that looked familiar, but she couldn't quite place why. The hostess pointed him to the table to the right of Samantha's booth. As the man passed by, his gaze landed squarely on Samantha's face.

"Ms. Spaeth, did you get all your brochures handed out?"

Now she knew who it was—Whitt Peoples, Diana's grandson. She hadn't thought she would ever see the stranger she'd met on the edge of Gulfview Boulevard again. He had been very clear he would not be attending the opening of her exhibit at the Historical Society.

"Yes, I think so," she said. "Now it's just a matter of wait–and–see."

"Kinda like Field of Dreams?"

"Field of Dreams? The baseball movie?"

"Yeah, you know, 'if you build it, they will come.'"

Samantha couldn't help but laugh a bit. "Something like that."

Before the hostess could lay Whitt's napkin on the table, words flew out of Samantha's mouth. "Why don't you just sit here?"

He hesitated a moment before answering.

Samantha could feel her blood pressure rising. What on earth had made her blurt that out? Why would Mr. Tall Dark and Brooding want to sit with a total stranger he'd tried to get away from just a few hours ago?

"If you don't mind. It's getting to be closing time. Probably makes it easier on the staff if they only have one table to clean."

Samantha felt her head stick at a curious, questioning angle. Her jaw dropped slightly, and she was unable to do anything about it. He was taking her up on her dumb, spur-of-the-moment offer?

"Or I can just go ahead with Plan A," he said, looking between the booth and the small table and chairs nearby.

Samantha shook the cobwebs from her brain. Could she look any more stupid?

"No, absolutely—you're totally right—I mean, I asked you first."

Yeah, because that made sense. She looked down at the phone she'd placed on the table. It had more than eight screens of apps she'd downloaded—and not one of them featured a button that could rewind time and make her not look like a grade-A idiot.

Stinking technology.

Whitt sat down and opened the menu. "So, what's good here?"

At least she could answer this question with confidence. Thank goodness. "Well, just about everything. But I came here for fried chicken and mashed potatoes."

"A comfort food kind of day, I guess."

She breathed a little sigh of relief. He got it. "Exactly. How'd you know?"

"I've had the same kind of day." He closed the menu without even studying it. "I'll take your recommendation."

"You won't be sorry about the chicken, but I am sorry to hear you had a bad day."

The waitress stopped at their table. "Y'all ready to order?"

Samantha gave her a tired smile. "Yes, I think we are. We'll both have the fried chicken platter with mashed potatoes and gravy."

"Lots of gravy," Whitt said.

"Got it." Their waitress made notes on her order pad. "Chicken platter, mashed potatoes, lots of gravy. It'll be out in just a few minutes. Do you want anything to drink with that, sir? I know you want your tea and lemons, ma'am."

"Iced tea sounds good," Whitt said.

"Lemons for you too? Or do you prefer sugar?"

"I haven't had sweet tea since I was a kid," Whitt said. As he looked at the waitress, a small smile crept across his face. "You can't get sweet tea in New York City. You get tea with a sugar packet, which doesn't count. I think I'll have one for old times' sake."

"Gotcha." She tapped her pad and turned for the kitchen.

"So how did you find the Down-Home Café? It's kind of hidden back here." Samantha was curious about a lot of things mysterious stranger, but she didn't want to come off like a total stalker.

Whitt unrolled the napkin around his silverware. "One of the nurses at the hospital told me how to get here."

"At the hospital?"

"Yeah, I'm here visiting a relative. Well, not exactly visiting. She's taken a turn for the worse, so I talk, but I don't know if she really listens. I don't know if she can listen anymore. They called me this morning and said it was probably only a matter of hours. They had to do some tests tonight, and the nurse thought it would be a good time for me to get out and get a bite to eat. I told her I'd be back in half an hour or so – and then I'll be there all night. I'll be there as long as it takes."

"Wow, I'm so sorry. So that's the death in the family you mentioned. I know that's a lot to go through." Samantha felt awkward. She felt like she should say something of value or comfort, but Whitt was barely more than a stranger to her. She was keenly aware that anything she offered had the potential to go terribly wrong, simply because she only knew him well enough to talk about things like the weather. However, it didn't take a psychologist to see that talking about the weather would come off as insensitive.

This man obviously had far too much going on to worry about the weather.

Whitt placed the napkin in his lap and smoothed it out four times in a row, brushing it over and over again until there were no folds or wrinkles in the embossed white paper.

"It is," he said with steely conviction. Silence settled around the booth.

Samantha heard faint laughter coming from near the cash register by the door. It sounded perfectly normal for every other meal she'd ever had at the Down-Home Café. But tonight, any laughter seemed utterly out of place.

"So, is this a family member?" She asked gingerly.

"My grandmother," he replied, with only a small hint of emotion.

Samantha's mind swirled a little bit. "Wait–your grandmother? When I saw you on Gulfview Boulevard, didn't you say Diana Peoples was your grandmother?"

At just that moment, the waitress reappeared with two glasses of iced tea. "Here's one unsweet with extra lemons, and one sweet tea. Your food will be out shortly."

She placed a straw alongside each glass. Whitt picked one up, stripped off the wrapper, and once he put the straw in his drink, he rolled the discarded white paper.

"She is."

Samantha could feel her blood pressure begin to rise several points. Diana Peoples was like a mentor to her. She was practically a mentor to the whole island community. "But I just saw her this afternoon. She was fine. What happened?"

Her chest squeezed tightly and her next few breaths put up a struggle.

"I have two grandmothers. Diana is fine. Well, as fine as she's ever going to be, I guess. I'm not here because of her. I'm here because of my Granny Kaye, my mother's mom." He laid the balled-up straw wrapper at the edge of his glass of sweet tea.

Samantha felt her shoulders slump with relief. Then guilt quickly swept in. She was glad to know the woman she held in such high esteem was still in good health. But Whitt's statement meant another member of his family was not expected to live much longer, and whether or not she knew this person, the news was still sad.

Before replying, Samantha took a moment to squeeze two wedges of lemon into her tea and collect her thoughts.

She thought back to their brief encounter earlier on Gulfview. Whitt hadn't wanted the brochure, hadn't been receptive to hearing Diana's name, and hadn't even seemed like he'd known about his family's role in Port Provident's history.

As a thought crossed her mind, she brushed it away for being rude. It seemed too nosy. It seemed too pushy for the current situation. Then the idea darted back, like an insect zipping toward a glowing light.

Instinctively, Samantha's hand waggled. She tried to brush away the bug-quick thought.

"Is there a fly?" Whitt asked.

Before she knew it, the words started to leave her mouth. "You don't seem to like Diana much."

Oh my gosh. She scolded herself immediately. What was wrong with her tonight? Samantha couldn't believe she'd just said that. The bug in her mind wasn't flying toward the glorious sun; it was headed straight for a zapper that would spell nothing but doom.

"I don't." He took another sip of tea, then continued speaking. "Actually, it's not that."

Samantha looked at him, confused. "It's not?"

"It's not that I dislike her. Really, it's not a question of whether I like her or dislike her. For me to care, she'd have to mean something to me. And she doesn't. Not anymore." Whitt looked down at his watch. "You know, I should probably just get my meal to go. I really need to get back to the hospital."

He waved their waitress over to the table and told her about his change in plans.

Samantha had no idea what to say as they finished waiting for their orders to arrive, so she picked up another lemon and squeezed it into her drink. She resolved to turn that tea into an Arnold Palmer—half tea, half lemonade—before she uttered one more word that would backfire on her.

They sat, squared off in silence, as a handful of minutes ticked past.

Whitt looked out the window at the black night sky. "So, is the weather always like this around Christmas? It seems rather warm for late December."

The weather. It had come back to this. He wanted to talk about the weather.

Samantha looked up from where she'd just been counting glittery sparkles in the ancient Formica tabletop, wishing she'd just steered the conversation to the boring old forecast to begin with.

Inadvertently, she caught Whitt's eyes with her own. His irises were dark brown, made even darker by the faded gold-toned lighting in the café. They reminded her of a cat she'd once had. Taffy had been an alley cat, one of those cats that tried to sass you with street smarts—until you realized it was all a cover for a deep desire to have a scratch behind the ears and a bowl full of crunchy food.

Whitt's snappy reaction to the observation about Diana was very Taffy-like. Maybe he just needed a scratch behind the ears. Samantha shoved the thought to the back of her mind. She didn't want to spend any time deciphering what her mind had meant by thinking that. She wouldn't ever see this man again—he'd attend to his family business and head back to NYC.

It was best to just stick with the weather.

"It was almost 80 degrees last week. But this time last year, it snowed. It goes to show you that all the adages about Texas weather are true."

The waitress walked toward them, holding a carryout bag in one hand, and a plate with a drumstick perched on top in the other. She placed the plate in front of Samantha and rested Whitt's to-go bag on the corner of the table. "Here you go. Thanks for coming in tonight. You can pay at the front, sir."

Whitt slid out of the booth and picked up his dinner. "Sorry I can't stay. I need to get back to my grandmother."

Samantha didn't believe a word of the first sentence, but she knew the second one was true.

"Merry Christmas," she said with no frills attached, believing that a holiday greeting was probably even more benign than a discussion about temperatures.

"Same to you. Good luck with your event."

"Thanks," she replied, but Whitt was already three steps ahead, walking toward the cashier.

During the year she'd spent planning for the new exhibit, Samantha had gotten to know many members of the Peoples family. Through research and exhibit curation, she'd gotten to know most of the family that still lived in Port Provident. Their ancestors had largely been responsible for the town's rebuilding almost a century ago after one of the nation's worst natural disasters.

But Whitt Peoples was definitely someone who had never made it on the Peoples family radar she'd seen—and judging by her limited time with him, he'd run into some kind of personal disaster in his own life. Something had made him break ties with his family; something had convinced him that his grandmother was the exact opposite of the woman Samantha knew Diana Peoples to be.

But what? Whitt Peoples and his past were more mysterious than any well-wrapped package under any Christmas tree in town.

Chapter Three

WHITT HADN'T PLANNED on heading back to the hospital so soon. Jeannie had told him it would take at least an hour to go through Granny's routine before the nurses switched shifts. But he'd rather sit on a curb and eat cold fried chicken than talk about Diana or any other member of the Peoples family.

Talk about an easy diet plan. Just thinking about that side of his family killed his appetite. If he belonged to a gym in town, he'd go there right now and take out his frustration in the free weight section.

Actually, he'd probably need a kickboxing class or something where he could pound out all the memories that kept popping up in his mind.

Too bad none of that was an option right now.

Whitt felt the buzz of his phone in his back pocket. He adjusted the take-out bag in one hand and pulled out the ringing rectangle with the other.

It was a local Port Provident number, according to the area code, but not one he recognized.

"Hello?" Whitt answered tentatively, half expecting that Diana Peoples had found his number or that Samantha Spaeth was tracking him down to finish their completely unpleasant dinner conversation.

"Mr. Peoples?" The voice was not his grandmother or his erstwhile dinner date. "This is Jeannie at the Provident Medical Center ICU."

He felt relief that it was Granny's nurse, but then his shoulders began to tighten, wondering if Jeannie was about to drop the bomb he'd been dreading all day.

"Hi, Jeannie. How's Granny?" Better to get the question out there so she didn't try to sugarcoat what was about to come.

Ice slid across the bottom of Whitt's stomach like a solid glacier. And just like he'd seen on every documentary about the Titanic, he knew there was so much more below the surface. He could allow himself the dread about what was to come right now—but eventually, he'd have to deal with the monumental significance of losing the last tie on earth to his mother.

"She's fine."

Whitt let out half a breath. Granny wasn't fine and would never be fine again. But "fine" was undoubtedly a better answer than the alternative.

Jeannie continued. "She's stable. I knew you'd said you were coming back after you had dinner, but respiratory hasn't had a chance to come do their work yet. I think she'll be ready for visitors again in about an hour. I'm about to rotate off shift, so I wanted to give you an update. I don't usually call patients' family members, but your grandmother is special. I thought she'd want me to let you know."

It warmed Whitt's heart a little to think that Granny had touched the lives of the people she knew, even in these last days and hours.

"Granny is special. I'll be back in an hour, then. I don't want to miss any time I have left with her."

The nurse's voice was so soothing and comforting that it almost felt like a hug was coming through the phone line. "We'll all miss Miss Kaye. I'm so glad you still have a wonderful grandmother in Diana, though. Both of my grandmothers have been gone for more than twenty years. You're very fortunate to have had as much time with both of these ladies as you have."

The temperature on the island had fallen considerably after the sun went down, and the briskness of the night air settled at the top of Whitt's lungs. Why did everyone keep bringing up Diana? She was nothing to him. J

Just as he'd been nothing to her or any of her extended family for most of his life. Whitt didn't want to discuss anything about Diana, even casually. He wanted to stay focused on Granny. She was the reason he was in Port Provident.

The only reason.

"I'll be back in an hour, Jeannie. I'll see you when you get back on shift tomorrow. Thanks for the call."

She replied, and they exchanged a few more items of information that Whitt needed to know about, then he disconnected the call and headed toward Provident Medical Center. He was a New Yorker—he didn't need to call a cab. Whitt could simply walk back and take a moment to himself. Things had moved so fast since he'd gotten the call early this morning.

Halfway down the block, Whitt stopped.

He'd forgotten to check into his hotel. The Grand Provident was long known for their giant outdoor tree and ornate decorations inside, so it was a popular destination this time of year.

It was only a few blocks away, so Whitt decided he would check in and eat his dinner in the room. He'd left his small travel bag in Granny's room at the hospital. He'd bring it back to the hotel later when he had another break like this.

When Whitt arrived, a jazz trio near the Christmas tree was packing their instruments back into large black bags. He could still hear the buzz of conversation in the open area bar off to the far-left side of the lobby, but otherwise, the marble-floored foyer seemed relatively empty.

He walked up to the dark wood counter.

"Hi, I have a reservation for Whitten Peoples. I need to check in."

The woman behind the desk was young—probably a student at Provident College, Whitt assumed.

She typed a few strokes on a keyboard, and then her eyebrows squished together as she studied the screen in front of her. "I'm sorry, sir, that reservation has been canceled."

Frustration rose through him like an elevator traveling toward a scenic observation deck.

"My admin just made it this morning. I've got a confirmation here."

Whitt placed his to-go bag on the counter near him, then reached for his phone. He started swiping with his thumb, searching for the email from his assistant.

"You did have a reservation. But we have a nine o'clock check-in deadline. When you didn't check in, we gave the reservation to someone else."

The clock on his phone glowed brightly in the dim light that filtered through the atrium area. It was nine-thirty-seven p.m.

"Okay," he said through a clenched jaw. "I'll just take another room. Bed size, smoking or non-smoking—none of it matters. I only need a place to sleep when I can."

The woman behind the counter shook her head without consulting her computer screen again. "I'm sorry, we are full for the night. I don't have another room to give you. Your room was the last one we had available."

That glacier-slow, cold sense of foreboding that had dogged Whitt for hours now shifted a few more inches. He couldn't shake it. He just felt the slow, but perpetual, motion and knew he couldn't brace himself against it. When it broke loose, it would create chaos and run over everything in its path.

"Nothing?"

She shook her head again. "Nothing. I'm sorry, sir."

He picked up the bag of chicken. There was no sense in arguing or trying to find another solution. Maybe this was his intuition telling him to spend the night in Granny's room, to spend that time with her.

That was probably it.

Gut instinct was rarely wrong. Like every other grandparent in the world, Granny had told him a hundred times or more that "everything happens for a reason" over the years. Most of the time—especially when it came to the circumstances around his mother's death—he wasn't inclined to believe her.

But tonight, he decided to honor those words that had come out of her mouth with such conviction so many times over the years. Whitt walked out of the Grand Provident Hotel and back toward Provident Medical Center.

He stepped outside into the dark night. The air felt as crisp as cold apple cider. To his left was a trash can, hidden by an intricately trimmed plant in an oversized pot. Whitt side-stepped and reached over, throwing away the bag of chicken.

Like just about everything else this evening, the cold chicken and congealed gravy was by now a complete waste.

WHITT LOOKED AT THE street sign on the corner. He'd certainly taken a wrong turn in his walk back to the hospital. The recollections of streets and neighborhoods he'd hung on to from his time as a ten-year-old boy on a bike—cruising this part of the island with the wild abandon of childhood—did little to help him now.

That's what he got for letting his mind wander down memory lane as he wandered down Port Provident's century-old sidewalks.

He kept moving down the block, hoping to find something that would jog his memory and get him back on track. If he didn't see something by the next corner, Whitt decided he'd have to concede defeat and check his phone's GPS-based map.

Light from a room above shone a faded yellow circle on the gray of the sidewalk. Whitt looked up at the house from which it originated. As his eyes adjusted to the shadows and trees obscuring the structure, he realized it wasn't a house at all. It was a garage, with an apartment on top.

He knew this garage apartment, knew this wrought-iron fence that stretched all the way to the stop sign ahead.

There were hundreds of garage apartments, situated on back alleys all across the historic housing areas of Port Provident. The small island was filled with one of the nation's oldest and most complete collections of preserved Victorian architecture.

This wasn't just any garage apartment, though.

This was Whitt's pirate fort.

The mental map left by that ten-year-old boy brought Whitt straight to the Peoples estate without even realizing it.

Whitt felt the corner of his mouth turn up into a faint smile. He was a bit like the Grinch, realizing that he indeed had the capability to feel. Whitt had never expected to see this place again. He knew he couldn't look over at the big house in the middle of the lot without feeling frustration—Diana would be inside.

But the garage apartment was different. The garage apartment was his. It represented one of the best parts of his childhood, a time and a place where his mom was still alive, and when he was unconditionally loved by a large, extended family. It was a place where his imagination ran free.

The gate to the driveway stood open. Whitt walked toward it, then kept on walking through it. He couldn't stop himself from seeing if it had changed through the years. As long as no one saw him, he could take a quick look, satisfy his curiosity—and then move on back to the hospital. Granny's treatments would finish soon, and then he could settle in that not-so-comfortable chair for a not-so-comfortable night of whatever rest would come.

A rustling sound came from the bed of a blue truck parked next to the garage.

The sound made Whitt stop walking. Before he could turn around and make his way back to the outside sidewalk, the man at the truck spotted him.

"Can I help you?" he said in a low tone with clipped syllables.

"I'm lost," Whitt replied. "Sorry, I'm leaving."

The other man took three quick steps and closed some of the gap between them.

"Wait a minute. Don't move or I'll call the police."

Whitt took a step back. "There's no need to do that."

"You're trespassing on private property. That's a gate over there. It might be open, but you obviously came through it deliberately. You walked a long way down this driveway to be standing here on accident."

The hairs on Whitt's neck stood up slightly. He could see something in the man's hand, but Whitt couldn't make out what it was. In the fading moonlight, Whitt could tell the man was someone about his own age and build. He figured he could take the guy if it came to that—but if that were a gun in the man's hand, this whole episode wouldn't end well for Whitt.

If the worst-case scenario played out, maybe he and Granny could get a double room.

Whitt shook his head—sarcasm didn't exactly become the situation. But thinking about Granny gave him an idea. Maybe he could buy just enough time to get out of there.

"I'm not trespassing," he said. "This is my grandmother's house."

"No, it's not," the response shot back. "It's my grandmother's house."

Well, that didn't go as planned.

Then, realization swept over him like a breeze off the Gulf of Mexico. "Jake?"

"Yeah? Who are you?" The man in front of Whitt shifted his weight to his right foot. "Wait. Whitt?"

"Yeah." His voice cracked at the end of the syllable as a lump rose unexpectedly in Whitt's throat. It felt like a snowball, lodged right at his vocal cords.

Without warning, Jake took off running straight for Whitt. Within seconds, his cousin was right there in front of him. There was no space, no distance of years.

Jake threw his arms around Whitt's shoulders and squeezed tightly. "Man...where have you been?"

Whitt swallowed, forcing the snowball to thaw just enough to get an answer out. "New York City—same place I've been for the last two decades."

"You never wrote back. I had no idea if you'd stayed there or had gone somewhere else or what," Jake said. He stepped back and sized Whitt up in the moonlight, then crossed his arms.

"I've been up there all along. What do you mean I never wrote back?"

"Don't you remember?"

Whitt shook his head. "I guess not."

"When you left, we said we would be pirate pen pals." Jake laughed a little, but his arms stayed crossed. "I guess that sounded cool or something at the time."

A memory gripped Whitt. They'd climbed the tree behind the garage apartment and exchanged a last round of secrets. Whitt had no idea it would be two decades before he saw his childhood best friend again. He'd thought he and his dad would come back.

"Probably. We loved pirates, didn't we?" Whitt struggled with the memories that were coming back to him in rapid-fire succession.

"We grew up on an island that pirates once roamed. How could we not?"

"Remember when we went to the fort down the road from the lighthouse?"

Jake nodded. "Oh yeah. We thought we were old enough to handle creeping around a supposed pirate hideout at midnight. We were wrong."

"Very wrong," Whitt laughed. "But you're also wrong about me not writing back. I never got any letters to write back to."

Jake had put his arms down at his sides. He crossed them back over his chest before speaking. "Yeah, you did. You sent them all back."

This time, Whitt matched Jake's pose. "No, I didn't. I don't know what you're talking about."

Jake turned slightly and pointed back at the garage apartment. "There's a box of them in there."

"What do you mean?" The snowball had long since melted, and licks of low fire were taking hold in Whitt's body. He felt almost certain that his long-lost cousin was calling him a liar.

"I kept them all. I wrote you a letter a week for the first year you were gone. You never wrote back. Then one day, I got a big envelope with all of them in there. They'd never even been opened."

A cloud fell over Whitt's soul. It wrapped around the innermost core of his being. He could feel the chill and whisper touch every thought, every question he'd had about his family for the past two decades.

Surely Jake didn't have his facts straight. It had been a long time.

Surely his dad would have told him if his cousin had tried to stay in touch.

Surely everything he'd thought about his family for all of his adult life was correct.

How could it not be?

"Can I see them?" Whitt asked the question with hesitation. He wasn't sure he really wanted to know, but on the other hand, he needed to see that it wasn't all made up—he needed to know they were real. Whitt had a few minutes before needing to be back at the hospital to keep watch over Granny during the night. Blood pounded in his veins—he knew he needed to use those minutes wisely.

Jake put out his arm, pointing toward the garage apartment. He took two steps forward and put his other arm around Whitt's shoulders.

Whitt looked up toward the main house, situated in the middle of the estate-sized lot. The light in the top back corner shone softly behind thin curtains. A woman's figure cast a gray shadow in the middle of the yellow glow.

As the cousins took their first step together, the light turned off.

"Absolutely," Jake said. "Welcome home, prodigal cousin."

HOO. BOY. SAMANTHA could feel every tendon, muscle, and bone in her foot. She could feel every tendon, muscle, and bone in the other foot. And then she felt a few more twinges that she would challenge even the best podiatrist to try to identify.

What a long day.

It had started before the sun rose. Reid Knight's TV crew arrived at the crack of dawn to begin their setup duties. Before lunch, she'd done interviews with the local paper, a glossy magazine focused on the island's lifestyle and tourists, and finally filmed a live vlog for the Historical Society's social media outlets.

Although hurricane season had passed quietly this year, a report had just come out that predicted an active season in the year ahead. People seemed to be more conscious of the future possibility right now. It had created a renewed interest in the Great Storm of 1910 and how Port Provident had rebuilt—and thrived—in the decades since.

Her afternoon then revolved around interviews with Reid Knight for his new series. Samantha gave him a guided tour of the new exhibit and other items of note in the history of her city. Then, it had been showtime. Thankfully, the house was packed, Reid got great footage, and everything went off without a hitch.

Now, she realized as she sat in a metal folding chair on the back row of the space they'd used for the dedication, she could just sit here and zone out. She wouldn't need to move until the

Home Sweet Home network crew finished tearing down the lights and pulling up electrical cords and a thousand other little things they'd set up for their coverage of the event.

She could relax.

For once today, no one needed anything from her.

"It looks like I missed the dedication," a voice said. It came from the direction of the doorway.

Samantha swiveled in her seat and saw Whitt Peoples, dressed in dark wash jeans and a black, fine-gauge sweater. In his hand, he held a well-crumpled brochure.

Her head was already dizzy from the helter-skelter day. Just the sight of him pushed her even further out of orbit. She'd like to blame it on the fact she'd only had appetizers and punch for dinner, but that wasn't it at all.

It was that darned black sweater, and she knew it.

Clearly, Whitt had never met a set of weights he didn't like.

Samantha shifted a little uncomfortably in her chair, now acutely aware of the fact she'd never met a set of gym weights she *did* like.

Good thing he wasn't in town long, or she'd tell herself that she ought to make a New Year's resolution about rejoining Island Fitness. And nothing had ever come of the ten previous years she'd told herself to do that. This year, she'd already decided to save her gym membership money and put it toward something useful—like pedicures.

"It ended about an hour ago. How can I help you, Whitt? I doubt you're looking for another dinner recommendation."

Thinking about how he stormed off from the Down-Home Café kept Samantha from thinking about how her extra twenty pounds really did need that gym membership. Plus, she realized, the righteous indignation that took up residence in her head had just given her a jolt like caffeine. Maybe it would help keep her awake until the HSH network guys were gone.

"I need your help."

"*Mmm-hmm*?" She couldn't think of anything more substantive to respond with. She tried to make it sound more like she cared by putting a high, questioning sound at the end of the syllable.

"I want to learn about my family."

"That's probably the last thing I expected you to say."

He didn't move from the doorway. He seemed as skeptical of his request as Samantha was.

"What did you expect me to say?"

She shrugged her shoulders. "'I'm sorry' comes to mind. You were a jerk at the Café, so I don't understand why you need my help. You've got plenty of family in town. You could ask them."

Briefly, he looked at his feet, then back up at Samantha. His eyes were as dark as wet sand. "I'm not there yet."

"Not where?" She adjusted her position and straightened her spine, trying to follow where he was going with this.

"I can't ask them. I don't even know them."

Samantha parsed Whitt's logic. "You don't know *me*."

"You're right. But you won't tell my father that I'm here. I think he deliberately kept me away from my grandmother and my cousins. But I don't know for sure. And until I know what the facts are..." He trailed off and paused as though he had gotten lost in thought. "I have to do this for myself—by myself."

She looked at Whitt, but this time she wasn't noticing the jeans or checking out the high-dollar sweater. She focused on his eyes.

They were dark. They were brown, but so deep in color that there wasn't much variation between pupil and iris.

Except... as she stared, she fixed her gaze on one small area of light like unfiltered honey near the lower right curve. It fascinated her because once she noticed it, she couldn't un-see it. It changed Whitt's whole face, made it softer.

The small spark made her see the child within. She saw a quick glimpse of that boy who'd had barriers put around him in order to buffer the events that he couldn't control.

She knew what that felt like. People had tried to define her with barriers her whole life.

She hadn't let them.

And she couldn't let them remain around Whitt if there was a chance to break them down.

She knew what her answer had to be.

"So, what do you want to know?" she asked.

Whitt nodded and took a step inside the door. "Everything. Let's start tomorrow morning."

"But what about your grandmother? Isn't she in the hospital? Isn't she the reason you came to town?"

"She passed away two hours ago. The Peoples family is the only family I've got left. That's why I need to know."

Chapter Four

"THE STORY OF WHO YOU are begins right here."

Whitt looked around him. All he saw was grass. Well, grass and a chain restaurant about a block and a half away to his right.

"In the middle of a field? That sounds like a scene from a bad romance novel."

Samantha scowled. "Seriously? You think I brought you out here to tell you some hot and heavy kind of story?"

Whitt raised one eyebrow slowly. "Well, maybe."

She rolled her eyes. "Ugh. Men. That is not it at all—"

"Might I remind you of how babies get made?"

"Stop it. Just stop."

Whitt leaned in a little closer, just to verify if he'd made steam come out of her ears or not. It had been less than twenty-four hours since Granny had died, but unbelievably, he felt like smiling. Samantha was taking his request so seriously—almost too seriously.

"Well, you said I begin right here. Apparently, you know something about my parents." He couldn't resist needling her just a little bit more.

He also couldn't help but notice she was cute when she got flustered. Her cheeks were red from the slight chill in the

December wind. It gave her porcelain skin a glow worthy of Rudolph's nose.

"Not your parents." Samantha stared him down. The clear daylight revealed her eyes to be a dark, mossy green shade. "Your great-grandparents on your dad's side. This is where they met. It was September 1, 1910."

A chill ran down Whitt's spine. He'd been a sarcastic jerk a second ago. He'd been trying to do anything to shake the sadness that had been chasing him since he'd arrived in Port Provident. And he'd used Samantha Spaeth's sincerity to do so.

He felt rebuked, almost as though his great-grandparents were still standing here, wagging a disapproving finger in his direction.

"What was here?"

"The Port Provident Children's Home. Remember when I met you, and then I gave you the brochure? We were just standing right over there."

She pointed to a spot about a block away, in the opposite direction of the chain restaurant he'd noticed earlier.

"You're right. I'd just been walking down the sidewalk there on Gulfview at the top of the seawall. I'd been trying to clear my head before going to see Granny. I don't think I really noticed where I was. I would have passed right by you if you hadn't said something to me first."

She laughed just a bit. "I'd set a goal to hand out one hundred brochures. You were number ninety-seven. At that point, I was handing brochures to anything that moved. If you'd been walking a dog, I'd have given him a brochure, too."

"I actually do have a dog. His name is Rufus. But he's at a kennel back in New York."

Samantha walked around the grassy lot. "Well, New York is an important key to part of your story. Ellis Island, specifically. John Peoples came to America from Scotland, and he did so through Ellis Island in 1904. By 1908, he was working here in Port Provident as a building foreman for a local architect, Walter Atchison."

Whitt looked out across the water. "So, I'm part Scottish? I never knew that."

"You're actually Scottish and German. John Peoples married a girl named Isabel Schuster. She immigrated to America from Germany about the same time that John did, only Isabel came in through Port Provident."

"She came in here? Why not Ellis Island? I thought Ellis Island was the big place for everyone to come through."

Samantha walked back over to where Whitt was standing. "Ellis Island is certainly the best-known port of immigration for America during that time, but people came *from* everywhere *to* everywhere at that period in history. Texas was a very popular place for immigrants to come through. Especially Germans. Think of towns like New Braunfels or Fredericksburg up in the Hill Country. There are pockets of residents who still speak German in those areas because the language has been handed down through the generations. The most popular port for those Germans to come through was right here in Port Provident."

Whitt couldn't believe he'd never heard any of this before. Listening to Samantha speak was like opening an encyclopedia and starting to read from A to Z. It felt as though he was just soaking up the little facts with every turn of the page.

"So, you said they met on September 1, 1910. How do you know it was that exact date? Is John Peoples that famous in this town?"

Samantha nodded. "Well, yes, he is. But that's not how I know. On that day, the Great Storm of 1910 rolled ashore. That hurricane would become the deadliest natural disaster in American history, and it almost wiped this town off the map. John saved Isabel and a little girl named Ingrid Buchholz that night."

"He saved them? Here?" Suddenly, the chill of the wind didn't faze Whitt. He needed to know more. He knew he'd stand out in the island's late-December wind all day if that's what it took to hear this whole story.

And as he looked at Samantha's dark green eyes, he realized he'd stand here even longer, for no reason other than to keep seeing the sparkle at the edge of the emerald iris.

"The Port Provident Children's Home stood on this site. Isabel Schuster grew up there after her father died of yellow fever. Her mother had already died in childbirth. Isabel was orphaned at twelve years old, and she and her three siblings lived at the home. She took care of a little girl named Ingrid Buchholz who had come to Port Provident on the same ship the Schusters had come on. Ingrid's mother died on the journey, and her father died in the same yellow fever epidemic as Isabel's father. On the night of the Great Storm, Isabel was nineteen and working as a teacher at the Children's Home. Ingrid was eight."

"So, they both lived here?" Whitt looked across the grassy rectangle. The land was flat. The grass was almost knee-high toward the back of the lot. Nothing gave away the significance of what had been here more than a century ago.

"They did. Ingrid was still a resident of the home, and Isabel had graduated. After she aged out, she stayed behind to teach the residents. She treated Ingrid like her own daughter—her diaries indicate that she had helped take care of Ingrid when she was a baby, when they were both on the boat to America, and still felt a deep attachment to the little girl."

"But what happened the night of the storm?"

Samantha reached into a canvas bag she'd brought with her. The side of the black tote bore the logo of the Port Provident Historical Society in white. The contrast of color stood out as sharply to Whitt as the details of this long-ago story were beginning to.

Samantha handed Whitt an old book. The cover was a brown fabric with the letters "MY STORY" embossed into the front. It looked like the letters had been golden at one time. He ran his finger over the surface. It was smooth and cold, and in an off-hand way, it reminded him of the place that surrounded him now.

"I thought I'd let Isabel tell you in her own words. She dutifully kept a diary every night, and although her diaries were destroyed in the storm, after the recovery, she wrote down her recollections about the Children's Home and the night of the hurricane, and her husband had them printed because of their importance. This was her actual copy, so you'll even see some of her handwritten notes she made after the fact. Diana donated this to us, and Isabel's story, told here, became the basis for the entire exhibit we just opened at the Historical Society."

Whitt walked back toward the edge of the lot and sat down on the curb. He rested the book on his knees and carefully opened it.

"You're saying my great-grandmother actually wrote this?"

Samantha nodded as she sat on the curb next to Whitt. She leaned in close in order to point at a page in the book. Whitt could smell Samantha's perfume. It lingered in the air with a soft, yet crisp note that reminded him of roses.

He leaned down to better decipher the faded ink where Isabel Schuster Peoples had added to the memories and descriptions which has been laid down in neat rows of type.

He caught a different scent of roses. Maybe that had been Isabel's perfume. Maybe she'd chosen to smell like a flower too.

Samantha skipped ahead a few pages in the slender volume. "This is where she starts to talk about the first signs of the storm."

The winds had come in strong from the north overnight, and I didn't remember seeing any force of nature quite like this since a squall hit our ship to America in my youth. Nevertheless, it was my duty that day to go into town for provisions. I knew it was going to rain—that much was clear. I prayed that God would get me to town and back before I was soaked. The wagon I took to town was open. A downpour would have ruined all the supplies I'd been asked to bring back.

I made four stops in town to get food for those of us at the Home. Next, Dr. Porter replenished our medical supplies, which were running low.

Then I picked up white fabric that had been on order at Mr. Bretton's mercantile. We needed to make new sheets for some of the beds in the girls' wing. The rain had begun to fall by this time, and Mr. Bretton begged me to stay in town until it passed, but I declined, knowing if I didn't return with our supplies, the children would not get a full meal at suppertime. If I hurried, I trusted that God would see me back safely.

John Peoples, the builder, was also in the mercantile, and he went out to my wagon and secured all my provisions. He echoed Mr. Bretton's sentiments, but I finally convinced him that the children needed me to return today.

I did not realize then that whether or not I returned to the Home, it would make no difference. There would be no more meals served at the Children's Home.

Whitt was used to being in charge. He was used to doing research. It was a crucial part of his job. He had to learn all the details of the clients he was considering working with.

Usually, details soothed him. They made sense.

But not right now. These details coagulated and brought a lump to his throat.

"Why were there no more meals at the Children's Home?" Whitt asked Samantha, but he feared the answer.

"Because by that night, there was no more Children's Home."

Whitt didn't move as he let the impact behind those words sink in. He knew hurricanes destroyed things.

"I lived the first part of my life here. I've always known about hurricanes. But I've only seen a few tropical storms and Category One hurricanes. They're wet and windy, but none of the ones I remember were damage makers. It's hard to think that something could be here for breakfast and gone by dinnertime. Have other hurricanes that have hit here been like that too?"

Samantha laid her hand over Whitt's where it rested on top of his great-grandmother's words. Whitt stayed still, feeling both the sadness in his heart for what had happened in this spot—and feeling a small measure of comfort from her gentle, soft hand.

"In some places. It's been a while since we've had a hurricane—knock on wood. I hope the predictions for next hurricane season don't come true. Rumors of active hurricane seasons always make me nervous. There are a few things I can still show you from hurricanes in the past. And of course, we have photos at the Historical Society. We have lots from both the Great Storm and other strikes that have hit the island."

"Could you show me?"

Samantha stood. "Let's go."

She took a few steps toward where they'd parked her car. Whitt stayed back for a moment, immobilized as he looked at a nondescript field that held secrets from more than a century ago.

"You okay?" Samantha asked over her shoulder.

"I guess things aren't always what they seem, you know? It looks like it's always been this way, like a parcel of land the city forgot. You know, if I'd driven by on any other day, I'd have assumed cows once grazed here, and that at some point, they'd build a big box store or something as the growth on the island outpaced the space available."

Samantha frowned. "They do want to build a big box store here. The land's been sold. We've been trying to negotiate with the company for years, trying to find some loophole to prevent it. Our local folklore says there's a cemetery here for people who died in the storm, but we've been unable to locate hard evidence. If we could, that would probably be enough to preserve it. According to a section of the Texas Health and Safety Code, once land is dedicated as a cemetery, it can't be used for any other purpose. But we haven't been able to confirm what we've been told, and now we're about out of time. We don't have any more cards to play. Next time you come back to Port Provident, the land where the Port Provident Children's Home once stood will be a Shop-N-Mart."

THERE WASN'T A SINGLE black dress hanging in Samantha's closet. Ten years ago, she resolved not to hide her light, and that included dressing to merely blend in. She'd decided that the world didn't have to like her, but they wouldn't be able to ignore her.

She'd been bullied and made fun of throughout school for being dyslexic. She grew up in a small town just north of Port Provident, on the mainland. The schools there were poor, and anything beyond the most basic of state requirements to help kids overcome disabilities was not in the budget. Everyone in situations like hers got sent to special education classes—and outside of the classroom doors, their peers brutally labeled them.

Not a day went by where Samantha wasn't called stupid or fat or ugly or any one of a hundred other taunts. Not a day went by where she wasn't turned away by some group or another at various lunch tables. No one wanted to be friends with a girl who was different, who struggled with the most basic principles of reading. She started to wear dark colors, just so she didn't stand out, and she hoped no one would notice her—or her disability.

The one thing no one had counted on was that underneath the superficial layers others saw, Samantha Spaeth was a fighter. The minute she shook off the dust of Montmorency, Texas, she enrolled for one class at Provident College. She took one class a semester at first and then found the help she needed. Through tutors and determination, Samantha earned her degree and found a job at the Port Provident Historical Society.

The day she walked across the stage in her black graduation robes was the day Samantha decided she was never wearing black again.

She would shine, and no one would stop her.

Well, at least not until God called her home, like He'd done for Kaye Vontegarten three days ago. She didn't know Kaye well, but had seen her singing in the choir loft at First Provident Church over the years.

But she had come to know Kaye's grandson, and she knew he'd be there at today's small funeral. Samantha also knew he'd be alone.

She quit looking through her closet for something she knew wasn't there. She grabbed a bright Christmas plaid dress and put it on.

It was the night before Christmas Eve—and besides, a woman who sang her heart out in a choir loft every Sunday for decades probably knew a thing or two about how to shine. Samantha felt certain that Miss Kaye would approve.

Samantha stopped in front of the full-length mirror and gave a little twirl, watching the flare of the skirt.

Her mouth curved up at the corners, and the woman who'd resolved to sparkle found herself hoping that Miss Kaye's grandson would approve too.

WHITT SHOWED UP AN hour early to the small chapel at the back of the First Provident Church complex. He didn't want to walk in with a bunch of people staring at him. Besides, he thought he'd like a few last minutes alone with his grandmother.

When Whitt first ran into his cousin, Jake had reassured him that he should use the garage apartment. He promised that everyone would leave him alone—if that's what Whitt wanted.

And since then, even though Whitt had slept under their roof—well, their garage's roof—the Peoples family had been true to their word.

It felt strange to have family everywhere he was here, but still to have no real connection.

Even though he'd been born in Port Provident, Whitt was a stranger in a strange land, and the only one who completely knew him and shared his memories was in the casket at the front of the room—where she'd become now just a memory herself.

Whitt stood silently, a half-step back from his grandmother, until tears formed in his eyes. He hadn't cried at his mother's funeral. He hadn't truly understood what death meant then. It had been a more abstract concept, interpreted through the eyes of childhood. Before his mother died, he hadn't even endured the loss of a pet. He didn't know then what it meant to lose someone forever.

He knew now.

The knowledge pushed against his chest until he thought his ribs would crack from the pressure building inside.

"I'd hoped I would beat you here," said a voice softly at the back of the chapel. "I didn't want you to be alone."

Whitt wiped his eyes with the back of his hands before he turned around.

Samantha stood just inside the doorway. The light from the vestibule surrounded her and made her plaid dress stand out.

In a flash, Whitt's mind zipped to the last Christmas season he'd shared with his mother, and a day a few weeks before the holiday when she wore a green-and-red plaid apron as they made gingerbread men to hand out to his teachers and friends at school. He hadn't thought about that moment in years. It made him feel as warm as the oven that baked those cookies so long ago.

Whitt did a double-take, taken aback by the memory. Samantha looked like Christmas. She looked like love.

His eyebrows raised. He'd just met Samantha. He'd noticed her eyes as they'd stood on the land of the Children's Home. He'd noticed her kindness the night she'd asked him—practically a stranger—to join him at dinner.

And now he'd noticed something else—but it wasn't just the plaid. However, he couldn't figure out exactly what it was.

"You look very festive." Whitt wished he could take that back. Now, not only could he not decipher what about Samantha made that pounding fear in his heart subside—he couldn't talk right, either.

She smiled, bringing more light into the dimly lit chapel. "I thought about Miss Kaye singing in the choir every Sunday, and I thought about all the First Provident Christmas concerts over the years—all those beautiful, traditional hymns that everyone loves so much. And I realized that even though I didn't know her that well, she'd brought me a lot of joy with her singing. I decided to celebrate that instead of to mourn her passing."

The light in the room filled the space in Whitt's chest recently torn apart by stifling pressure.

"You said you didn't know her well, but I think you just summed up what she'd have wanted."

Samantha's shoes tapped on the tile as she walked down the chapel's aisle.

"Good. Can I sit here?" She gestured at the seat next to Whitt's. "Is that seat taken? If you're expecting family, I can find another spot."

"My mother was an only child. I'm not expecting family today. Just a few of Granny's friends. I think it will be a short service."

Samantha walked past him, and the cool smell of roses followed in her wake as she laid her purse on the padded pew.

Before he had a chance to get past any small talk with Samantha, the sound of more footsteps filled the room. Whitt looked back toward the doorway and saw Diana. Behind her was Jake, holding hands with a dark-haired woman. She was visibly pregnant and held the hand of a toddler with dark ringlets and dark eyes. The little girl was almost the spitting image of her mother. Behind them was another woman with sandy hair and three children. She turned and said something to the man behind her.

It took Whitt a moment, but then the realization hit him. That was Jake's sister, Jenna.

He'd come to the chapel early to be alone. He'd stood up by Granny and felt sorry for himself about having to return to Port Provident, a place that felt so hollow to him.

And then, like the lightning-quick speed of Santa's sleigh, he'd found himself surrounded by family and friends, both new and old.

"We thought we'd come early so you wouldn't be alone." Diana broke the silence that had given Whitt free-rein with his conflicting thoughts. "Of course, you talked to Jake the other day. This is his wife, Gracie, and their daughter, Gabriela. And then, this is Jenna and her husband, Mitch, and their three children—Jacob, Jennifer, and Joanna."

Whitt raised his hand in a half-wave. He didn't quite know how to handle the Peoples family coming out in force.

He looked at Samantha, who smiled at the group. "Do you think you'll all fit on the front row with us?"

Diana and Jenna's family filled out the rest of the pew. Jake and his family sat immediately behind Whitt. Directly in front lay Granny Kaye, his last link with the past.

Just like that, Whitt was surrounded. Those who came did so because they cared. Not just about Kaye, but about Whitt. They'd all said as much, leaving no room for doubt. Whitt let his shoulders settle, releasing the tension he'd built inside.

The rest of the guests flowed in and took their places, talking in hushed tones. Within a few minutes of the chapel filling, the minister began to speak about Kaye's life and her impact on others.

"The Bible tells us 'blessed are those who mourn, for they shall be comforted.' But I think all of us in the room here know we are blessed beyond that. We are blessed by the years we spent with Kaye Vontegarten and the years we will spend with our memories of her."

Whitt didn't know what he'd been expecting from the remarks at this funeral, but he hadn't expected that they would lighten his spirit. He hadn't expected to feel comforted—yet, just as the scripture had said, Whitt knew that's what he was feeling.

Comfort.

For the second time in two days, Samantha reached out and covered Whitt's hand with her own.

This time, he tucked his fingers back and connected with hers. She gave his hand a gentle squeeze back.

He'd spent his whole life running from Port Provident because that's what someone had once told him he needed to do. Maybe he'd been moving in the wrong direction all along

Chapter Five

SAMANTHA HADN'T PLANNED on attending the graveside service, but Whitt seemed comfortable with her presence with him through the long afternoon.

More than that—if she hadn't known better, she would almost say he'd enjoyed her presence during the afternoon. He'd included her in conversations, looked her straight in the eye as he said a few words during the eulogy, and he'd continued holding her hand throughout the service.

Now, as the sun began to sink into the December sky, Samantha found herself wishing for the toastiness that had been generated between their hands.

Or...maybe just a pair of gloves. Gloves would have been cheaper—and far less perplexing than Whitt Peoples.

Off to the side of the tent that the cemetery had erected at the gravesite, Whitt shook hands with one elderly couple.

"I'd heard her tell the stories of you and my grandfather in the Coast Guard. I know she would appreciate that you traveled here today. Thank you for coming."

The emotion in his voice wasn't sadness or wistfulness, it was simply straightforward gratitude. He'd taken the time to talk to every single person who'd attended today—even the members of the Peoples family.

Finally, no more friends or family remained. Dusk had started to settle and cast shadows around the elaborate above-ground crypts that dotted the cemetery's rows.

Samantha stood at the far back of the tent, unsure of whether she should stay or go. The moment seemed quiet, private—and she didn't quite feel like it was her place to be.

"Wait just a minute. Please, Samantha?"

Whitt's words made the decision for her.

He walked to the closed casket and placed his hands on the lid. She could hear him saying his final goodbyes, but she couldn't make out the exact words. Carefully, he leaned down and rested his forehead on the curve of the ice-gray metal, then after a pause, he turned and gave it a kiss. With a final, solid pat of one hand, he left his last message behind.

"Rest in peace, Granny. I loved you more."

Samantha heard his words clearly, and the strings of her heart snapped with a pop, like a wishbone in a holiday turkey.

Whitt walked over to Samantha with a purposeful stride. He seemed to be using deliberate actions to keep his composure in check.

"If you don't have any other plans, I'd like to take you to dinner."

She felt the corners of her lips raise slightly, but shook her head. "It's been a long day for you. You don't need to make it any longer on my account."

"I'm not going home to anyone, Samantha. I'd like to thank you for being here today. And I owe you a real meal with pleasant conversation—not a stressed-out grouch who took his plate away in a take-home container."

He smiled a tired smile at her, and it made his eyes turn a shade as warm as a mug of cocoa. She never could turn down cocoa. And apparently, she couldn't turn down Whitt Peoples, either.

"Okay. I'd like that."

"Is Porter's Seafood still open?"

"It is." Samantha's mind wandered. She saw visions of a plate of stuffed crab and rice pilaf alongside a salad with house-made honey pecan dressing.

"Would you like to go there? We used to celebrate my mom's birthday at Porter's every year."

"Sure. It's not far." As they walked across the grass to Samantha's serviceable sedan, Whitt placed a hand under her elbow.

"This ground is pretty uneven," he said.

Samantha kept putting one foot in front of the other. She had worn low, wide heels, so she wasn't having trouble walking, but she made no move to shake off Whitt's support.

She needed what bracing she could get.

Because regardless of the state of the grass below her feet, Samantha was sure she was walking into uncharted territory.

IT DIDN'T TAKE LONG for them to get to Porter's and get settled at a table. Whitt had specifically requested a window seat, and luckily, there was one available. Across the street, the Gulf of Mexico churned. The water was choppy tonight.

Whitt studied the view. "What do you think Isabel and the others thought as they saw the sea rising?"

Samantha tapped the front of her bag. "We actually know what they did and thought. She captured it all in her narrative about the evening. I brought the book today. I got permission from Linda Pershing, the exhibit's curator. She said you could borrow the book for twenty-four hours if you wanted to read it."

Whitt turned back toward Samantha as she pointed at the antique volume. She saw a spark in his eyes that reminded her New Year's was just around the corner.

"You did that for me?"

"I was happy to. You said you wanted to learn who you were, where you came from. I happen to have some of the keys."

The waiter came and took their orders.

"I'll take the stuffed crab platter." Samantha folded the menu and handed it to the man. He was wearing a crisp white shirt and a tie with the red Porter's Seafood logo. She looked back at Whitt and laughed. "I've been thinking about it since the minute you said you wanted to come here."

Whitt smiled. "I can't decide. I'll take the Provident Platter. It looks like there's one of everything on there."

"A great choice, sir." The waiter made notes on his pad. "Would you like your flounder grilled or pan-fried?"

"Tonight's not the night to play it safe. Let's make it pan-fried."

A quick shiver ran up Samantha's spine. *Tonight's not the night to play it safe.* Whitt had been talking about fish, but her mind ran somewhere completely different. Samantha thought back to standing in front of her closet earlier, looking for the dress society wanted her to wear to a funeral. She remembered all the years she had played it safe.

Then, she'd cast off the external façade all that stuffiness represented and had stepped into the bold, bright colors that better summed up who she wanted to be.

Although she'd changed so much in so many ways since leaving her hometown, in one respect, she remained the same old Samantha. She had transformed herself from a girl who'd been bullied into a woman who could make a friend in any room in which she chose to walk.

She had made herself someone who lived without fear.

Except in one area.

She still never let anyone get close enough to lose her heart. When it came to quiet dinners with charming men and all the steps that came afterward, she'd always played it safe.

Tonight's not the night to play it safe.

Whitt Peoples would be leaving for New York again in a day or two. He had made a cool détente with his family, but they weren't close by any means. She doubted he'd ever be back in town. After tonight, she'd probably never see him again.

Why play it safe? Why not allow herself just the smallest taste of the one thing she knew she'd never have? A guy like Whitt Peoples would never be interested in a woman who still got letters confused and who needed to lose twenty pounds and worked at a job because she loved it, not because she had any chance of advancement.

She wasn't a New York City woman. She was one hundred percent Port Provident, a hometown girl.

But maybe for tonight, she could quit playing it safe and just pretend that like Isabel Schuster, she'd found her one true love when she least expected it.

WHITT COULDN'T BELIEVE he could laugh so much after a funeral. Somewhere around the time that the waiter brought them a plate of sautéed shrimp crostini, Samantha had flipped a switch.

Her steady, graceful presence had been just the quiet support he'd needed since the moment she walked into the First Provident chapel, but as dinner went on, she told anecdotes about town leaders, stories about the recent taping with Reid Knight and the Home Sweet Home network, and most interestingly, stories about his family.

Apparently, Diana and Jake ran the Peoples Family Foundation, and in that capacity, they regularly interacted with the Historical Society and Samantha's department.

She relished filling in all the quirky details, and Whitt had unexpectedly eaten it all up, just as surely as he'd eaten one pan-fried flounder, half a dozen fried shrimp, two stuffed shrimp, one stuffed crab, and two perfectly seasoned southern hushpuppies.

Samantha had insisted on the bourbon pecan pie for dessert, and Whitt worried that if he ate another bite, the next time she made him laugh, he was going to split a seam on his one good pair of pants in Port Provident.

As Samantha pulled her car to a stop in the driveway leading to the garage apartment, Whitt realized he didn't want the evening to end. Most nights in New York, he worked until he couldn't keep his eyes open—then he got up, went into the office and did it all again the next day. If he was honest about himself, he was a workaholic who didn't get out to have much fun, and he had few true friends.

And he had even fewer evenings full of laughs.

He wished there was a way to make this one last a little longer before he took a flight back to his dull reality.

"Want to take a walk with me?"

"Outside?" Samantha wrinkled her nose. "It's in the thirties out there."

"That's practically summer in New York City."

"I'm a Texas Gulf Coast girl. My blood is a little thinner than that of your average New Yorker."

Whitt unbuckled the seatbelt that had him safely strapped in the front seat. He reached his arms behind and tugged at the sleeves of the jacket to the suit he'd been wearing all day.

"Here's a jacket. Now please say yes."

Her hesitation filled the front seat of the small car like a cloud blowing in off the coast. She turned her head and looked him squarely in the eye. As she did so, Samantha's entire expression changed.

"What do I have to lose but a few toes to frostbite?" She wiggled a bit and slipped the coat on over her dress, then turned off the car and grabbed her small purse and her bag.

They walked down several blocks when an octagonal building caught Whitt's eye. Someone had draped twinkle lights inside around the perimeter of the windows.

"What's that?"

"It's called the *Blume Gesellschaft*. It's owned by the Historical Society now. It was donated to us about twenty years ago."

Whitt walked through the decorative metal archway that led to the parking lot in front of the unique structure. As he got closer, he saw that the building was green, but paint in a stencil-like floral pattern accented the trim. It reminded him of buildings he'd seen on a trip he'd once taken with his father to the Alps.

"This is charming. Has it always been here?"

"*Mmm-hmm*. Since 1892. It's one of the few structures on this part of the island that survived the Great Storm. The Peoples Estate is obviously another one."

Whitt took the short set of stairs two at a time and peered in the windows, studying the room in the dim glow of the twinkle lights. "What was the name again?"

"*Blume Gesellschaft*. It means 'Flower Society' in German. In 1890, the town's German citizens organized the Port Provident Flower Society, and they bought this land and turned it into a park. A few years later, they built this building as a meeting hall for their social club."

"You can almost imagine an oompah band playing right over in that corner." He pointed toward a raised stage at the back."

"There was a Christmas party booked here tonight. I bet they filled it with music and dancing a few hours ago—just as it would have been more than a century before." Samantha dug in her purse and then slid a heavy brass key in the lock. "I can't believe you spent a decade of your life in this town and have never been inside one of our most beautiful buildings. Luckily, I have a key on my work key ring."

The heavy wooden and glass door swung open. As soon as they were inside, Samantha pushed the door back in place and leaned on it until it let out a small *click!* sound, then she turned the lock back.

"So, this place survived the Great Storm, but the Children's Home didn't?" Whitt walked around the hardwood floor and studied the details on every angled wall.

"It did not. I told you that John and Isabel met that night, but we haven't had a chance to read more of Isabel's recollections of what happened."

Samantha sat on the edge of the raised stage. Whitt sat alongside her, then found himself scooting closer as she began to read.

There we were, huddled together in the stairwell, singing the new song "His Eye is on the Sparrow" over and over again. There were no birds out in the great wind that blew all around, so we hoped that instead, He would turn his eye to us. It was black as midnight in the middle of the home, and we heard the great thump and crack as objects flew into the walls outside.

Over the chaos, I kept hearing a rhythmic pounding which sounded unlike any of the other noises which surrounded us. Ingrid said she thought someone was knocking at the door. I knew it was impossible, but when the sound continued, I slipped away from the group to investigate.

Ingrid was correct. Somehow, John Peoples had made his way to the Children's Home from his place in town. He said the water was rising, and we needed to move all the children to the attic. He gave a last look at his horse as the sheets of driving rain pounded down. He did not even bother to tie the horse up. Perhaps free, the horse could run somewhere and survive. Tied to anything, the horse's fate would surely be sealed.

I saw Ingrid standing on the stairs, waiting for me, and all of a sudden, a gust of wind blew through the door and knocked all three of us flat. "Get up, get up," John said. "We must get higher."

I did not bother shutting the door. I could not have found enough power to close it, nor did it seem that it would matter. We ran up the stairs as fast as we could. As we passed the girls' dormitory, John stopped. Seeing the bolt of white cloth I'd bought earlier at Bretton's, he grabbed it and ran to the scared huddle gathered on the landing. We worked quickly, wrapping the cloth around the waists of the children and tying them together like human knots on a rope. When we ran out of the cloth, we grabbed bedsheets. Then he took one last set of bedding and tied Ingrid to me and tied me to him. "Get to the attic," he said. I followed his lead in the dark. Then we sat, huddled together and waited.

"We need to pray," John said. And so, we did—over and over and over until our throats were sore.

Whitt shivered. The *Blume Gesellschaft* suddenly became a freezer, bitingly chilled from the haunting echoes of the past.

"What happened to them? You don't have to keep reading. Just tell me."

She closed the book and closed her eyes, telling the story from memory. "Not long after that, the roof blew off the Children's Home. Once the roof was gone, the walls broke apart. History tells us the storm surge in the area rose to more than twenty feet, and most estimates agree that the winds at the height of the storm would have been close to two hundred miles an hour. There's never been anything like it in American meteorological history since."

Whitt tried to swallow, but his whole mouth had gone dry. His tongue stuck like Velcro to the roof of his mouth. "And the children? And the teachers? Did they survive?"

Samantha opened her eyes, and the golden reflections of the small white lights around them danced across the glassy surface of her deep green irises. "One teacher and one child survived. And one brave man who'd risked his own life to save a woman he'd just met that afternoon at a store. John Peoples later said that anyone who would turn down the offer to remain safe to head back to certain danger deserved his respect. He said the instant he met Isabel Schuster, she had not only earned his respect but had stolen his heart."

"So only Ingrid, Isabel and John survived?" Whitt took a labored breath.

"They were found the next morning. The sheet remained still tied around them, and it had gotten wrapped at the top of a tree. That's what saved them."

At that moment, Whitt knew John Peoples was not the only member of his family who had been saved from the storm.

"All my life, I've lived in a storm," Whitt said, quietly. "The day my mom died, my dad changed. It was an accident. She had an asthma attack in her sleep. No one could have prevented it. But he didn't care. I don't know why he blamed everyone, but he did. I've always known I was born in Port Provident, but I didn't really know where I came from until tonight."

He put his hand over Samantha's, just as she'd done earlier at the funeral. He felt the gentle curve of her hand, and it gave him strength. It gave him hope that his life going forward didn't have to be the same as it had been in the past.

Whitt scanned the room, wondering what he could say to thank Samantha for the insight she'd helped him unearth—without saying something that would make her think he'd gone crazy. As he thought, the flicker of the dim lights reflected off a string which somehow dropped from the high, central point of the ceiling. The skinny wiring ended with a flourish of greenery and ribbon about eight or nine feet over the floor.

He slid off the raised platform and tugged on Samantha's hand as his feet hit the floor. She went at an angle and lost her balance as she landed. His arms wrapped around her and held her up. She felt as soft as a cloud in the angle of his elbow, and his heart beat noticeably. Instead of the tightness that had filled his chest earlier, now he only felt adrenaline pushing him to do the one thing he couldn't get out of his mind.

He guided her to the center of the room and steadied his hands, one on each of Samantha's shoulders. He felt the seam across the shoulder of the suit jacket she still wore. He pressed his hands as he slid them down her forearm, then reached around her back and pulled her closer.

To his surprise, she didn't pull back.

He tilted his head, calling attention to the ribbon-tied bunch above them. "Mistletoe," he said. "I owe you a kiss."

Leaning in quickly, his lips met hers, and instantly, the sparkle and twinkle was not just limited to the strings at the perimeter of the room—it was inside his veins, and it made his arms pull her just a little closer. He wanted to know she was real, to know that the reason he no longer felt the December chill was because they had set a small spark off between them.

When at last the kiss was over, she tried to take a step back, but Whitt kept his arms locked tightly around her. She studied his face but didn't say a word.

"The moonlight and mistletoe made me do it," he said.

She pulled her hands up and placed them on either side of his face as she looked above.

"Look. It's still there." A white puff of her breath floated between them. She leaned forward and grazed his lips with her own as she finished her train of thought. "My turn."

Chapter Six

THE CLOCK HAD LONG since struck midnight when Whitt and Samantha returned to the driveway alongside the Peoples Estate. As Samantha drove away, Whitt noticed the back light at the top floor of the house was still on, just as it had been the night he'd been confronted by Jake in the driveway. About fifteen minutes later, as he searched the small garage apartment kitchen for a snack, he heard a light knock at the door.

He went down the flight of stairs that led to the door and looked out the small window.

Diana stood out in the overnight chill, wrapped in a dark brown wool coat and a fuzzy scarf. She held a few books next to her chest.

"May I come in?"

Whitt gestured for her to go up the stairs. For one, he couldn't deny her access to her own guesthouse. And secondly, for some reason, he had no desire to. He was done putting up barriers.

"It smells like popcorn."

The microwave beeped as they reached the living room area.

"I was hungry. I hope you don't mind that I grabbed something out of the pantry."

"Why would I mind? Besides, that's probably Jake and Gracie's popcorn. They're the last ones who put anything in that pantry." Diana frowned a bit. "Does popcorn have an expiration date?"

Whitt emptied the bag into a bowl and salted it. "I don't think popcorn does, but I know something that needs one."

"What's that?" Diana's voice bore a hint of hesitation.

"Whatever this is that's been between me and you and the rest of the family for years."

She pulled out a chair around the small kitchen table and sat down, placing the books to her right. Whitt noticed a slight sheen of tears in the corners of both her eyes.

"I agree. This has gone on long enough. But what's made you change your mind?"

"You," he said, without hesitation. "*You* came to the hospital when I was there with Granny. *You* offered me a place to stay. *You* brought everyone to the funeral today to support me. If you'd had anything to hide, you wouldn't have done any of that."

"I came because I love you. It doesn't matter to me how far away you went or how long you've been gone or how many of Jake's letters you never opened. You're my grandson. I still love you."

"Nana," he said. The word caught in his throat. He hadn't called her that to her face since he was a kid. "What happened? Why did we move? I never got any of those letters Jake sent. Why would Dad send them back unopened?"

The years peeled away. All of a sudden, he was ten years old again, looking out a plane window, searching as hard as he could for the outline of Provident Island through the clouds. The memory felt like ice as it replayed in his mind.

"Your dad blamed me. That's it plain and simple."

Jake felt his eyebrows squeeze together. He questioned Nana's statement. "You? Mom had suffered from asthma since she was a kid. You didn't cause her asthma."

"No, but that afternoon, we'd been down at the beach flying a kite with you. Your mother would have spent all day, every day at the beach if she could have. We ran around and played and just generally had a wonderful, silly time. None of us knew it then, but that triggered her attack later that evening. I was the last person besides you to see her alive. Your father blamed me—and he wanted to get away from me, from the beach, from everything that reminded him of Julie's death."

"And me," Whitt admitted.

"I don't think he wanted to get away from you, Whitt."

"He worked all the time. He was never around. He spent all his time preparing for one big case or another."

Diana reached into the bowl and grabbed a handful of popcorn. "I think he thought winning those cases would bring him the resources he felt he needed to give you what you'd lost."

They chewed the white fluffy bites in silence for a moment.

"How could any amount of money make up for losing a mother?"

"It can't. And I would have told him so if he'd asked me—but he never asked me. He's never really asked me anything since you both left town."

They shared more popcorn and more quiet reflection on the years that had passed them by.

"But you'd forgive me this easily for holding a grudge against you all these years?" Whitt didn't know quite how to ask the question that was on his heart, so he just threw the words out there in an ineloquent fashion.

"Why wouldn't I want to be a part of your life if I could? You're my grandson. I've prayed for you every day since you went away. And no matter where you go or what you do, I'll pray for you every day until I meet Jesus myself."

Whitt finished the last handful of popcorn. "I know you believe in all that prayer stuff, Nana—and based on what the pastor said at the funeral, it seems like it was important to Granny too. But I've never seen it work. Prayer didn't bring my mom back, and it didn't make my dad happy. And believe me, I prayed for both of those until I saw what I asked for just didn't matter."

Diana stood up from the table and scooped up the books. "Come with me."

He followed her into the living room. She walked over to a bookshelf and pulled out a slim antique book much the same size as the one Samantha had shared with him earlier. Instead of being brown, the cover of this one was a faded red.

"The Perils of Port Provident," Whitt read the title on the cover. "Oh, the Great Storm. Samantha showed me a book about it—about John and Isabel and that little girl."

Diana opened the book about halfway and thumbed through a few pages until she found what she was looking for. "Read this chapter title," she said.

"John Peoples Prays to Put Port Provident Back on the Map," Whitt read.

Diana nodded. "The power of prayer. It's been evident as long as our family has been in Port Provident. Don't think it doesn't apply to you. I showed this chapter to Jake, too, once when he needed to see it. John Peoples prayed for an answer to help rebuild his town. He used his skills and knowledge as a builder to design homes that could be built quickly for the citizens of Port Provident. He saved this town because he knew where his help came from."

Whitt sat on the sofa behind him and read the first page of the chapter.

"He prayed in the attic, too, didn't he? When he went to the Children's Home to save Isabel and the other girl?"

"Mm-hmm," Diana said as she sat next to Whitt. "That's what the story Isabel wrote said. Having married his son and knowing the man for many years, I have no reason to doubt it. And without all those prayers that night, you wouldn't be here. You're their legacy, Whitt."

He remembered the story that Samantha had read to him, the tale of fear and of hope.

"It's not just the Peoples family, though. Ingrid Buchholz married Wilhelm Vontegarten about ten years after the storm. Their son, Markus, died before you were born, but he married a lady I think you know well."

"Granny?"

"Yes, Markus was your grandfather. The story of the Great Storm really is your story, Whitt. It's the story of people who were able to survive extraordinary circumstances and do extraordinary things. You belong here in Port Provident, and I'm glad you came home, even if it was just for a while."

She reached out and hugged him tightly. Whitt felt a wet trail down each cheek.

Whitt forced past the lump in his throat to say the words which needed to be said. "I love you, Nana."

"I love you too, dear boy. I brought you these books. They were your great-grandmother Ingrid's. Kaye gave them to me a while back to donate to the Historical Society, but I had always hoped to show you first. Kaye had a number of antiques in her estate she wanted to donate. Maybe you can sort through them before you go home."

"I'll do that tomorrow."

Diana tried to cover up a yawn. "I guess it's past my bedtime."

"Let me walk you back to the house, Nana."

Whitt accompanied her to the back door of the mansion his family had called home for more than one hundred years.

As he walked back to the garage, Whitt looked at the sky. The moon had risen high and looked as crisp and white as a giant glowing snowball in the sky. A sprinkling of stars reminded him of the lights of *Blume Gesellschaft* earlier tonight—and that kiss with Samantha under the mistletoe.

When he'd arrived in Port Provident, Whitt had thought he was going to lose everything this Christmas. Maybe he'd been wrong.

Maybe he was going to find everything he never knew he'd been looking for.

SAMANTHA SAT IN HER office. It was Christmas Eve, and all she could think of was how much the Grinch must have loved her current predicament. The developer was ready to break ground on the Shop-N-Mart just after the start of the year.

The book Isabel Schuster Peoples had written was on the corner of Samantha's desk. She reached out and touched it lightly with the tip of her pointer finger.

"I'm sorry I failed the children, Isabel," she whispered. "I just can't tell where they were buried—if it's on this plot of land, or somewhere adjacent that already succumbed to so-called progress long before I came on the scene."

A knock at her door shook Samantha out of her depressed train of thought.

"Come in," she said.

Whitt Peoples stuck his head around the edge of the door. "I think I have something you'll be interested in."

Samantha looked straight at Whitt's mouth. She'd be interested in another trip to the center of *Blume Gesellschaft*, but that probably wasn't what he was talking about.

"What's that?" She tried to pretend like she was thinking about something far more business-appropriate than kissing Whitt Peoples.

"Ingrid's diary. There is no official cemetery."

Her mood slumped again. "That's what I pretty much figured."

Whitt walked up to Samantha's desk and flipped open a feather-delicate book with neat handwriting in faded ink. "Your answer is right there."

She twisted her lips into a sideways pout. "Where? I don't understand any of that."

"It's German," Whitt said.

"Right." Struggling through English had been enough of a challenge. Taking on foreign languages would have been out of the question during her school days.

"The children were buried where they were found." He ran his finger along the lines of small script as he read. "And then there's a diagram on the next page."

He pointed at a drawing of a rectangle. Numbers were scattered around the shape. On the opposite page, each number had a name written on it.

"Those are the children's names. Thirty-seven children were buried there, but not in a cemetery. That's why you haven't been able to find records. And according to Ingrid's diary, the town treated it like a sacred burial ground, even though it was never formalized. That's why it's been kept aside all these years."

Samantha couldn't believe what she was reading—or more accurately, what Whitt was reading to her. This was the missing link.

"Texas courts have ruled that they require no special record to have been filed to dedicate a cemetery—only that land was used as one. We have to get this to the county."

Samantha jumped out of her chair and ran to Whitt, throwing her arms around him as soon as she reached him.

"I can't believe this!" She leaped up and gave him a short, exuberant kiss. Then she realized what she'd done. "Wait. No mistletoe. I'm sorry. I got carried away."

He put his hands around her waist and picked her back up into the air. "No apologies necessary. It's a celebration."

"Indeed, it is." She leaned her head forward just a bit to see if he'd take the hint.

He did.

Samantha's blood pressure did a cartwheel, a flip-flop, and a spirited high-five all at the same time.

When the kiss was over, her brain resumed function and spit out a laundry list of questions. "When did you find this? Where did you get Ingrid's diary? When did you learn German?"

"Last night—or rather, early this morning, from my nana, high school... in that order," he replied with equally rapid-fire.

"How does Diana have Ingrid Buchholz's diary? Ingrid basically disappeared after the storm. We know she survived, but not much else."

"She moved to the mainland to live with distant family for a few years, then returned to the island after marrying a man named Wilhelm Vontegarten. You attended their daughter-in-law's funeral this weekend."

A mild form of shock washed over her. "I had no idea. I don't think any of us here at the Historical Society did."

"So... what do we do next? You said you've got to talk to the county?"

"Right. They're the ones who decide these things. But they're slow. Hopefully, we can get an injunction or something."

A slow grin spread across Whitt's face. "You should call Reid Knight. A company like Shop-N-Mart will not like the publicity of destroying the final resting place of children who died in a national tragedy. It'll play right into the piece he's already filmed."

Samantha's eyes grew wide. "You're a genius. A really mean genius."

Whitt nodded. "It's kind of what I do professionally, in a way."

The brakes slammed down on Samantha's adrenaline. She hadn't known Whitt for long, but it felt like she had. Maybe it was because she knew so many details about his family and the generations that had come before him.

It had given her a false sense of security. He would leave—maybe even today—and go back to his life in New York, then she'd be here with her memories of the day she decided to stop playing it safe and dance under the mistletoe.

"What is it?" he asked. "You don't think the county will get things straightened out in time?"

"No, no, it's not that." Her heart sank so low that Samantha felt as though she could step on it.

"Then what is it?"

"When are you leaving?"

"The day after tomorrow. Nana asked me to have Christmas dinner with the family, and I couldn't say no. But after that, I guess it's back to reality." He rested the diary on Samantha's desk. "I'm going to leave that with you, though. Use it to get the designation you need and then just give it back to Nana."

She swallowed hard, trying to break up the lump in her throat. She'd never allowed herself to think Whitt *wasn't* returning to New York, so Samantha couldn't understand why her heart was acting like this conversation revealed anything other than what she already knew. They didn't have some sort of instant love—like how John Peoples knew he had to go after Isabel after only meeting her once.

Samantha promised herself she would not cry in front of Whitt Peoples. She would only allow herself to do what she'd done for years.

She would shine.

She would be a strand of twinkle lights.

She would be a glass Christmas ornament on a tree.

She would be the white glow of moonlight filtered across the floor of an octagonal building that kept the secrets of the last century.

"We'll take good care of it. We'll keep it safe."

As she said that, Samantha tucked her heart back in the box where it had lived, undisturbed, for so long.

Samantha would keep it safe too.

WHITT SAT AROUND THE table for a Christmas unlike any he'd been accustomed to for most of his life. Usually, he and his father went to a restaurant in Manhattan. They ordered prime rib and then went back to the brownstone and opened practical gifts like sweaters and fountain pen sets.

This was completely different. The boisterous sounds of children filled the room. The familiar tear of gift wrap came from behind the twelve-foot-tall Christmas tree in front of the bay window.

"Girls!" Jenna raised her voice. "Get out from behind that tree. I'll tell you when it's time to open gifts. Nana is going to read the Christmas story. Come sit on the couch."

Gabriela, Jake's daughter, sat next to Whitt. As Nana began to read from the oversized family Bible, she leaned her toddler-sized body against his and snuggled right against his side. There was a lot he'd come to love about New York while he'd lived there. But even though the world assumed New York had everything, it didn't have this.

Family.

People who would pray for you.

People who opened their arms and welcomed you back into their circle.

People who helped you know where you came from. People who shared in your memories and were there to help you make more.

As Nana talked about the wise men following the light of the star, Whitt's mind wandered back to the light of the moon through the windows at *Blume Gesellschaft*. When the wise men had set out on their journey, they hadn't realized what they would find. The same had proven correct in his own life, Whitt realized.

He'd come back to where he was born in order to be a part of the end of something.

He never dreamed that he'd actually discover the beginning of who he was.

Nana finished telling the tale that had rung true for thousands of years, then invited everyone to join her at the table for the Peoples family Christmas dinner.

As Whitt followed cousins and children and other family members he barely knew into the dining room, his phone vibrated in his back pocket.

He looked at the message on the screen.

Merry Christmas, Son.

How typical of his dad to send a text to wish him a Merry Christmas. Before he could reply, another text box popped up on the screen.

Your Granny's will has left everything to you. Call Morton, Harrison and Dunlop–they're a good legal firm that can help you take care of it. That way you don't have to stay in Port Provident.

Whitt stared at his phone for a moment, then replied.

Merry Christmas, Dad. I think I'll take care of it myself.

Without hesitation, Whitt walked to Nana in the dining room. "Dad just texted me, and now it seems I need to take care of something. Go ahead and eat—don't wait on me."

Nana looked surprised but took Whitt's announcement in stride. "You'll miss the wishbone, but we'll save you a plate."

"I'm through wishing, Nana. Maybe you could just say a prayer for me." Whitt felt nothing but gratitude for the woman who'd held him in her heart during the long years he'd been away.

She gave him a smile as jolly as one from St. Nick himself. "I can always do that."

"Thanks," Whitt said. He plucked a sprig of mistletoe out of the elaborate Christmas decoration near the door as he passed by.

As he walked outside, he pulled his phone back out and sent one other Christmas text.

Where are you? I have a Christmas gift for you.

Working, the reply came back. *Victorian Christmas Dinner at the 1892 Kellner House on Avenue L.*

Whitt consulted the map feature on his phone, which showed he wasn't too far from the Kellner House, a sizeable turn-of-the-century house in the Palm Court historic section of town. With each step, he thought about his life back in New York. He thought of the first-class restaurants. He thought of his apartment that offered a glimpse of Central Park. He thought of the buzz he got from meeting with new clients and talking about big ideas that might just change the world.

And as he turned the corner of Avenue L, he thought of John Peoples—a man who *did* change the world simply because he had faith that the impossible could be done. He believed he knew the woman he'd spend the rest of his life with the moment he saw her, believed in racing into a storm when no one else would, and believed in the power of community.

But most of all, John Peoples believed in the power of a love so strong it transcended wind, waves, and weather.

Whitt opened the door to the Kellner House. It swung open quietly and smoothly on well-oiled hinges. He peeked around the frame of the door. The dining room and the parlor area were joined, and one long, formal table stretched between them. About twenty-five or so people were seated around it in their Sunday best. A fire crackled in the fireplace, and a traditionally decorated Victorian-style Christmas tree stood bedecked in the corner.

No snow had fallen to the ground in Port Provident, and the local weather report forecast the temperatures to be near the mid-fifties for the day. It was hardly the stuff of Christmas carols, yet Whitt could have sworn he walked straight into a Currier and Ives painting.

As he closed the door behind him, Whitt stood in the entryway, not wanting to make a scene. He hadn't seen her at first, but then she leaned over to speak to the man seated next to her. Her blonde hair had been twisted and curled into an elaborate hairstyle that looked like it belonged below a tiara. Her shoulders were bare, and the heart-shaped neckline of her wine-colored velvet dress set off the glow of her skin.

Samantha caught his eye and gave a brief nod.

He would wait. He would wait as long as it took to talk to her, to tell her what he'd been thinking about on the walk that brought him back to her.

Whitt tried to use the brief moments to collect his thoughts, but instead, he decided to catch his breath as Samantha stood from the table. Whitt counted his good fortune as he took a moment to take in the sight of her, fully dressed in Victorian holiday finery. She met him in the entryway.

"Merry Christmas, Whitt. Did you come to say goodbye?"

"No, not exactly. I came to do a little business."

She tilted her head and gave him a questioning look. "This isn't New York City. In Port Provident, we take time for our friends and family on Christmas Day. The business can wait."

He shook his head. "Not this business."

"Okay." Her reply sounded skeptical.

"There's been a change of plans."

"We had plans?"

Whitt took a deep breath. This wasn't going the way he'd envisioned it in his mind. He was talking to a Samantha he didn't recognize. The woman he'd gotten to know listened to her heart and spoke her mind.

The woman he'd kissed in the moonlight lived as though she believed in all the possibilities that could be.

"We might."

She pointed at the assembled room behind them. "I've got a table full of guests I'm entertaining, Whitt. I need to get back to them, and you need to get back to New York."

"Not really."

"Yes, really. These are some of the biggest donors the Historical Society has, and we come together every year for a traditional holiday meal. I can't just leave them."

Whitt finally relaxed and broke into a smile. He'd gotten her in a catch-22. "So... you do work on Christmas."

"These people have become my friends. We share common interests and goals. Besides, we don't all have Manhattan apartments and Manhattan salaries," she said.

"I understand," Whitt said, brushing off the frosty tone in her words. He could tell she'd decided to keep him at arm's length. He wished he knew why. "But since you're sort-of working, I'd like to do a little bit of business. I'd like to formally donate the full estate of Kaye Vontegarten, and the diary of Ingrid Buchholz Vontegarten that I left with you, to the Port Provident Historical Society."

Samantha's jaw dropped slightly. "You'd like to what? But how?"

"It seems Granny left her entire estate to her only grandson. And I'd like her things to remain where they belong—as part of Port Provident's history." Whitt smiled as the light came back to Samantha's emerald eyes.

"So that's your plan?" she said, with a hint of hesitation.

"Not all of it. My plan is to take you to dinner at Porter's Seafood any time you decide you'd like to eat stuffed crab. And then my plan is to hire a band and dance with you in my arms all night at *Blume Gesellschaft*. And then my plan is to watch the sun rise over the water every day and thank God that I left behind my life in New York for the place where my roots run deep, and my story still has yet to be written."

"Wait. Are you saying that you're staying for a while?"

"Hopefully long enough to write my own history in Port Provident. Would that be alright with you?"

Samantha reached out her arms and Whitt pulled something out of his pocket. Holding high the sprig of mistletoe he'd drawn from the arrangement at Nana's, he gathered her close and leaned in.

"But first, my plan begins with this. Merry Christmas, Samantha. Here's to many more memories. Here's to many more kisses under the moonlight and the mistletoe."

Epilogue

REID KNIGHT CAME BACK to Port Provident at the end of the start of the next fall. The grass waved green and tall in the field where the Port Provident Children's Home had once stood.

"You're the CEO of Shop-N-Mart, a global retailer known for aggressively pursuing business opportunities," he said to the man standing next to him. "What made you decide to turn your plans around and work with Port Provident to put a park in at this property instead of a store?"

"Well, it was actually this man here," he said. "He showed me the importance of this site and that we could both achieve goals if we worked together."

Reid threw his next question to Whitt. "This is an unexpected partnership between a corporate giant and a small non-profit. How did it come about?"

"Before I moved to Port Provident, I'd worked with start-up businesses to find unexpected angles to drive their success. When I learned about the impasse between the city and Mr. Sullivan's company, I put that hat back on and looked for solutions, and we found one. Shop-N-Mart's corporate social responsibility program often focuses on their suppliers—they help create better packaging and reduce the carbon footprint of getting the products in their stores. But in this case, we found a way for them to partner with the Port Provident Historical Society by donating the land back to the city to create this park and historic site. We've clearly displayed signage and have other ways throughout where we've recognized them as our main sponsor, while still preserving the integrity of the site. We're thrilled that we've been able to partner in this way."

Samantha watched as Whitt handled the interview with skill, and she was delighted that she'd been able to get Reid to come back to town to film a follow-up on the feature that he'd shot on Port Provident's Great Storm exhibit. That piece had launched his now-successful show.

But most of all, she was thrilled with how this vision for preserving this piece of history had come together so quickly under Whitt's leadership. He used his negotiation skills, paired with the resources from his family's foundation to pull it off. Each grave had been carefully marked and preserved. A network of sidewalks twisted through the site, and the landscaping had been selected to reflect the original garden design that had once been planted around another city landmark, the *Blume Gesellschaft*. Everything here reflected the deep, rich history of the island. Signs throughout told the story of the Great Storm, and near the center, the Historical Society had built a replica of the Children's Home for visitors to tour.

None of this would have happened if she hadn't handed a brochure to a stranger on Gulfview Boulevard last Christmas.

Whitt wrapped up his interview and walked back to Samantha. He put his arm around her, and she felt complete contentment as they stood together watching people learn about Port Provident's history.

"Come with me. I have something I want your opinion on," he said.

"I hope it's not the forecast. You should ask Reid Knight about that. I'm just glad we got this opened before that thing in the Gulf gets too big. Looks like we're going to get some rain next week. It would have been so disappointing to postpone this project."

"Nope. I'm not thinking about that at all. The last report shows it headed up towards New Orleans. Besides, who's afraid of a storm named Hope? She's probably too polite to even break out of Category One."

They walked, hand in hand across the site, back to the newly built replica of the Children's Home.

"Instead of weather reports, I've been thinking a lot about this place," he said.

Samantha gave a short laugh of understanding. "You've worked eighteen hours a day for the last two weeks to make sure the park was ready for today's opening. You've planted flowers, nailed boards and done just about everything else in between."

"Well, I've had to. This is my legacy. We're standing right where my great-grandparents met. If John Peoples hadn't blown through the first doorway that stood here on that September day in 1910, Isabel and Ingrid would not have survived. Without John and Isabel and Ingrid, I wouldn't be here. They're all a part of my story. And I never knew they existed until I met you. That makes *you* part of my story."

Samantha started to speak, but Whitt laid a finger across her lips.

He got down on one knee just in front of the door and pulled out a ring from his pocket.

"Samantha Spaeth, will you help me write the rest of my story?"

Many years ago, she'd resolved to shine. But never until now, Samantha realized, had she truly glowed. Her heart filled so full, so fast, that she could barely get the one word out she knew she needed to say.

"Yes!" The world stopped spinning as Whitt slid the ring securely to the base of her finger.

"There's one more thing," he said.

Samantha couldn't keep her eyes off the ring. What more could there possibly be?

Whitt took out his wallet.

"You don't have to pay me to marry you, Whitt." Samantha attempted a joke as she tried to figure out just what her fiancé was doing.

Without a reply, he pulled out a small rectangle of white cloth from inside the wallet and unfolded it. In the center lay a small, dried green sprig. Gently, he lifted it above their heads.

"No matter where we are or what time of the year it is, promise you'll always kiss me under the mistletoe."

This time, she didn't need even one small word to reply. She just leaned in and let her heart shine.

You Don't Have to Leave Port Provident!

Start Labor of Love Now!

GLORIA GARCIA RODRIGUEZ has always cherished her independent streak—an approaching hurricane and she has one very pregnant patient are proving to be more than she can handle. Evacuations ahead of the storm mean that the only person in Port Provident Gloria can turn to is Chief Rigo Vasquez—the man she holds responsible for the death of her husband. Gloria's desperate phone call opens the door for Rigo to make things right with his first love, but will his labor of love to keep Gloria and her patient safe be enough to rebuild their future once the storm passes?

https://books2read.com/LaborOfLove

Join Kristen's Reader Community Today and Receive a Free Port Provident Story

Join Kristen's reader community today for the latest and get A Place to Find Love, *a sweet escape romance that introduces you*

to Port Provident, Texas and the residents who find love on the island, for free!
www.kristenethridge.com/newsletter[1]

Sneak Peek: Labor of Love—Chapter One

IN LESS THAN TWENTY-four hours, Hurricane Hope would be too close for comfort to Gloria Garcia Rodriguez's island home. If it weren't for this sudden change in the storm's path, she never would have ventured to one of Port Provident's worst neighborhoods—somewhere she didn't choose to go even in broad daylight. And now with the gray clouds rolling in, casting the pallor of dusk around corners and throwing shadows on the ground, she welcomed her task even less.

On Monday, the Texas Gulf Coast looked in the clear.

On Tuesday, forecasters said the mass of clouds churning in the Gulf of Mexico had wobbled to the west.

And now, on Wednesday, the red line of the hurricane tracker drew a bull's-eye for Port Provident, Texas. If everything stayed on track, it would be here soon. The swirl of violent weather was too close and moving too fast.

Gloria walked up the narrow steps that led to the landing in front of apartment L5 and noticed the rust on the handrail

---

1. http://www.kristenethridge.com/newsletter

and the peeling green paint along the wall. The worn-out building depressed Gloria as much as the thought of the impending hurricane. How would a building that appeared to be on its last leg on a sunny day fare when a major storm pounded it? Gloria didn't hold out much hope for the future of the small, dilapidated apartment complex or the residents and possessions inside.

She'd tried her phone to reach Tanna DeLong, a midwifery client due to give birth any day now, but there'd been no answer.

With the hurricane bearing down on Provident Island, Gloria knew she wouldn't be able to rest easy or evacuate herself until she'd ensured all her expectant moms were off the island and had a contingency plan in case they went into labor while evacuated.

Gloria easily reached the other two moms who were close to their due dates. Both planned to shelter with relatives in Houston, which was close enough for safety while traveling, but still far enough away to escape the brunt of the storm. There were plenty of hospitals nearby where either of those mothers-to-be could reasonably expect to be taken care of, should the need arise.

On the other hand, Tanna was younger—only nineteen—and didn't have family to take care of her. She'd come to Port Provident six months ago after fleeing an abusive boyfriend in Georgia. Apartment L5 was technically leased to a friend who'd offered Tanna a couch to crash on. At yesterday's checkup, though, Tanna shared with Gloria that her friend was picked up by the Port Provident Police Department on a drug charge and hadn't been home in two weeks.

Tanna was all alone, except for the baby in her belly. As a midwife for the past decade, Gloria always felt responsible for the safety of the mothers in her care, but somehow she felt unusually protective of young Tanna.

Gloria knocked at the door and waited for it to open, but it never did.

She knew Tanna had to be nearby—her red compact Chevy sat in the parking space closest to the stairs. She knocked again, and the thin wood quivered a bit under the force of Gloria's hand. The door opened slightly, the safety chain still connected at the top of the door. Tanna's left eye was barely visible, but not much more.

"Gloria? What are you doing here?" The voice from behind the door sounded unsure.

"The hurricane is coming and I need to make sure you're safe. All my other patients have evacuated. You're the last pregnant mama on the island and we've got to get you out of here. Can you open the door?"

A warm breeze whipped up and slapped Gloria in the face, a small sign of what was to come in the next few days.

"Get out of here? Where am I supposed to go? I don't have anywhere to go." She started to shut the door. Gloria quickly stuck her hand in and gripped the frame.

She reached up for the safety chain and poked it with a finger. "Undo this and let me in so we can talk, Tanna. We'll figure out something, I promise."

The crack in the door narrowed a bit. Gloria tried to figure out how she could wedge herself in the small space. She couldn't let Tanna cut herself off like this, not with her first labor and a hurricane coming together on a collision course.

"Tanna, please. Don't..." Gloria stuck her hand in the space and prayed Tanna wouldn't slam the door shut on the now-vulnerable fingers.

A scraping noise came from just above Gloria's head, and then the chain dropped free. The door opened just enough to allow Gloria a tight passage around her very pregnant patient.

"Oof. I'd really like to just go lay back down, Gloria. My back is killin' me."

"Your back? Upper or lower?" The door closed swiftly behind Gloria.

"Lower. Like right here." Tanna pressed the top of her pelvis with her fingers. "I can't get comfortable."

Gloria had seen the start of labor more times than she could count. Normally, it didn't faze her at all—it was just part of the whole process. But the average first-time mother in her care spent around fourteen hours in labor.

And according to the news reports, fourteen hours from now, Port Provident would be engulfed by Hurricane Hope.

Gloria took Tanna by the hand and led her to the couch. "Come on over here, Tanna. Let's talk. Tell me more about how you're feeling."

The young mother-to-be moved a small cushion behind her back and sat down cautiously. Still holding her hand, Gloria sat next to her and asked a few questions about what Tanna was feeling and for how long.

Tanna's water hadn't broken yet, but after observing her and timing things, then doing a quick check of dilation, Gloria made a very certain diagnosis.

"Honey, those aren't cramps. Those are contractions. You're in labor. It's still early and we have some time, but that's a definite rhythmic and measurable pattern you've got going there. I'm getting you out of here." Gloria reached in her purse for her cell phone.

"So we're going to the clinic?" Tanna's eyes darted, quick and catlike.

Gloria felt empathy for her. It was a lot to process.

Gloria did some processing of her own and furrowed her brow. "Well, no. The clinic is closed. It sits close to Gulfview Boulevard and Dr. Shipley was very concerned about flooding later."

She thought about calling the paramedics, but this wasn't an emergency. And it was far too early to take Tanna to the hospital. Women in this early of a stage of labor were sent home to wait and progress. Thanks to the imminent hurricane, she didn't know what to do. But she knew she had to do something. Thankfully, she knew people who would know the best options. Maybe instead of going to Provident Medical, which would surely be understaffed tonight, someone could get them an escort off the island and she could get a hospital in Houston to admit Tanna a little earlier than usual, in light of the circumstances.

Gloria pulled out her cell phone and dialed a number she knew could bring help. It rang four times before going to voice mail.

"Tanna, go pack a small suitcase with whatever you need. We're both going. Now. I know people."

She scrolled a little further through her contacts list.

Straight to voice mail.

Three more numbers, three more recorded messages.

Gloria was running out of numbers in her phone to call.

Gloria scrolled through her list again. Maybe she'd overlooked someone.

Well, there was one number she could call. She just hadn't planned on ever calling it again. In fact, she couldn't believe she hadn't deleted it out of her phone two years ago.

Gloria's fingers felt shaky as she connected the call. The phone stopped ringing and Gloria's best hope for saving Tanna and her unborn child answered. "Vasquez."

Although she hadn't spoken to Rodrigo Vasquez in longer than she cared to remember, his short salutation made time stand still, and Gloria realized she knew his voice almost as well as she knew her own.

"Rigo, it's Gloria. I need your help." There was no time to catch up, which thankfully meant they wouldn't have to discuss the night her husband died or why Rigo shut himself out of her life shortly thereafter.

"Gloria." Rigo paused. "Wow, it's been a while. What do you need?"

He didn't hang up on her, so that was a start. Even though merely rediscovering his number in her contacts list made her shake with fear and memories, Gloria knew calling Rigo was the right move. She had to do whatever it took for the health and safety of her patient—even if it affected the safety of her heart. Quickly, in her mind, she prayed he wouldn't leave her all alone again, not at this moment when she needed official help so badly.

"I need an escort off the island. I have a client in labor and I need to get her some place safe before the hurricane gets here."

"I'm in the beach patrol division now, Gloria, not back on regular patrol with Port Provident PD."

"Your aunt told me that at church a few weeks ago. But no one else is answering their phones and I can't call 9-1-1 for this, not with a hurricane on the way. I figure a first-time mom very early in the first stage of labor isn't an emergency priority, not with water already rising in the streets."

"No, you're right, it's probably not. I was headed to check on a report of surfers on the west end—no one's allowed in the water today. But I'll radio Davis. He can go issue their citation and I can be to you in a few minutes. Where are you?"

"In the Gulf Air Apartments on Avenue R. Apartment L5."

"On my way, Gloria—I'm close. Those apartments aren't even safe. You shouldn't be there to begin with. And they're not going to make it through the hurricane unscathed. Those units are owned by a slumlord and have been falling apart for years."

Through the phone, she heard the siren on Rigo's truck begin to wail. "That's why I called you."

"Tanna?" Gloria called down the small hallway of the dingy apartment. "Are you ready? It's time to go."

IN HIS YEARS PATROLLING a beat around the streets of Port Provident, Rigo Vasquez had been through some of the island's seediest crack houses, had shot criminals and had wound up with a few holes of his own, and ultimately watched as his best friend and patrol partner died.

But he'd never felt the slick, icy fear running through his veins like he did now, knowing Lieutenant Felipe Rodriguez's widow waited on the other side of the door at the top of the stairs.

Rigo looked around. The parking lot seemed completely silent—no one walked around and no cars were pulling in or out. Even so, Rigo's hand slid across the handle of the gun in his holster that he still got to carry as the new head of Port Provident's Beach Patrol, a division the police force that wasn't just responsible for lifeguards and water safety, but also for keeping the island's beaches safe and mischief-free. Whenever his hand made that subtle shift, no matter how ordinary things looked, Rigo knew to trust his instincts.

Something wasn't right here.

And he was actually thankful. At least that sense of impending danger kept his mind off what he was about to do.

Face Gloria for the first time since the night his carelessness took everything away from her. Rigo knew he could never give her back her husband or her unborn child, and his gut squeezed tightly at the bitter memories.

But if he kept his focus and did his job, maybe he could get her out of here safely.

He owed that much to Felipe.

He owed that much to himself.

At the top of the stairs, the heavy feeling of instinct intensified, and he flipped open the holster to his gun. Instead of just touching the metal, he wrapped his fingers around it and slid it out. He couldn't shake the sense of being watched. Rigo pulled the gun up and held it steady as he investigated, walking from one end of the porch to the other. Everything seemed clear.

Still, it was time to get Gloria and her patient and get out of here because Hurricane Hope was picking up speed faster than any forecaster had predicted.

As unsettled as he felt about facing Gloria, he felt even more unsettled about the hairs on the back of his neck continuing to prickle.

He needed to do his job and quit thinking about the past. Gloria might be his partner's widow, but he needed to treat her like any other citizen of Port Provident.

"Gloria! Open up." He knocked on the door with his free hand, still gripping his weapon in the other.

Rigo felt his mouth go dry as he saw Gloria for the first time in almost seven hundred and thirty days. Not that he'd been counting. She'd changed, yet still looked completely the same. Her hair used to come down to her shoulders, but now it fell in layers just past her chin. It seemed lighter, too, with more honey than mocha. But with the summer days just now fading away, he figured that was the work of hours spent with sun and sand, not a salon.

Or maybe it was just the glow of the yellow bug light overhead.

He looked past her into the small, dark apartment. Noticing her hair was okay, he figured, but Rigo didn't want to see her eyes, didn't want to remember all the tears that he'd put there time and again. He wanted to get her and her patient to safety, tell himself it made up for the years of pain he'd caused and go back to his carefully orchestrated plan of quietly making amends while living separate lives on the small island.

"You ready?" He turned his head slightly left, then slightly right, telling himself he wasn't avoiding Gloria, he was just being careful.

"Yes." She let out a soft breath, like a feather floating away on the breeze. He wondered if she'd been holding it as she listened to his footsteps come up the stairs.

"Tanna? Come on, honey, we've got to go." Gloria's eyes darted around and she surveyed the landscape with a wary look, then she put her arm around a slightly built, very pregnant teenager. A scuffed-up suitcase rested at the girl's feet. "Felipe will keep us safe."

She'd called him Felipe.

He didn't think anything could have hurt more than two years ago when the ER physician came out to tell him that his lifelong best friend, his partner on the force, was dead. But now he knew he'd been wrong.

It was hearing Gloria call him Felipe.

It was knowing that he couldn't protect Felipe then, he couldn't protect Gloria now and he couldn't protect his heart ever.

"Rigo. I meant Rigo," Gloria said as they stopped in front of his beach patrol truck. She looked up at him, then just as quickly looked away. "This hurricane has me distracted. Thank you for coming when I called."

"Gloria, you know I'd do anything for you."

She stared at him, unblinking.

"So where have you been the last two years?"

She never missed a beat, and she was clearly still as direct as ever.

Rigo took a breath and stared into his cupped hands. He just wanted to get her and the young mother in his truck and get out of there, but he knew he owed her an answer that had already been put off for two years.

"A couple of steps behind, Gloria."

"What? I had no idea what your answer would be, but I at least expected it to make sense."

He promised himself a long time ago in a poorly lit, practically bare room that he wouldn't run from his past anymore. He wanted to break that promise. Badly. But he'd already broken too many promises where Gloria Garcia Rodriguez was concerned.

"I've been around, Gloria. I've just tried to stay out of your way since I've been back in town."

"Are you saying you've been avoiding me?"

Rigo shrugged. "It hasn't been coincidence that you didn't see me, Glo. But it hasn't been some ulterior motive, either."

"Then what is it?"

Rigo opened the door to the backseat as he tried to choose his words carefully. He hated that his concentration was divided like this. If the situation was serious enough that Gloria felt she needed an escort from law enforcement, he needed to give it his full attention.

But he couldn't just go through the motions when it came to Gloria anymore. She had hard questions and they were equally deserving of his undivided attention.

Silently, he and Gloria worked together, helping the heavily pregnant girl get inside the backseat of the truck. The rain began to fall more steadily from the solid wall of gray overhead.

"It's complicated, Gloria." He could feel the left corner of his mouth twist bitterly. "Can we just leave it at that for now? The only thing you need to do is get out of here and off this island. You still have about half an hour before they close the causeway. This isn't the time to conduct an interrogation."

She started to say something, but Rigo raised a hand and cut her off. "Not that you're not the best I've ever known at it. The CIA should have posted a recruiter at your door before you went to nursing school. They lost out."

Gloria rolled her eyes. "I don't know about that."

"I do. I know a lot about you, remember?"

Rigo's mind did a quick rewind past recent history and stopped on a sunny day in the late spring almost fifteen years ago. *Had it really been that long?*

In his mind's eye, he could see a version of the woman standing in front of him now, with hair teased a few inches higher and lipstick a few shades brighter. She stood at the end of the baseball dugout at Provident High School, just before practice was about to start. His arms wrapped around her waist, and he could almost feel the softness of her curves again under his tight arms, muscular from hours in the weight room and swing after swing that sent baseballs flying over the outfield fence. He remembered her saying something completely serious about where they'd be in the future, and as usual, he'd laughed it off.

"Glo...I've told you a thousand times. You're not going to be happy taking over your parents' restaurant. You just need to be around babies. Lots of them." He leaned down and kissed her lightly on the mouth, teasing her out of her scowl and back into a smile. *"Preferably mine. After I make it to the big leagues, you can stay home, knee-deep in being a mom, and we'll pay someone to take over the restaurant. Just because being a madre is a traditional role, it doesn't mean what's in your heart is less valuable than being some big-shot career woman. Just be who God made you to be—and He didn't make you to be a restaurant*

owner. Don't let anyone tell you what's in your heart is wrong. Trust me. I know you. I know you better than you know yourself, Gloria Garcia."

"Maybe you do, Rigo. Maybe that's why we'll be together forever."

Gloria got in the truck without any assistance from him and Rigo pushed the daydream away like the windshield wipers he'd been using all afternoon. He forced himself to gain control of his thoughts, to put them back into the here and now. Gloria had called Rigo today only for Tanna's protection.

Not her own.

He could only assume she'd been honest about dialing his number because she didn't have any other options right then. She didn't call because she needed him in her life.

Felipe's death was in the past. Felipe and Gloria's son's final breaths were in the past.

And Rigo Vasquez needed do his job, take Gloria and her client back to Gloria's house so Gloria could collect a few belongings and get off the island.

Once he knew they'd be safe, Rigo knew where he needed to go—back to Gloria's past.

Keep reading Labor of Love

Click here: https://books2read.com/LaborOfLove

Want to extend your stay in Port Provident?

Start a new book now!
The Home to Love Series
Language of Love[2]
Legacy of Love[3]
Labor of Love[4]
The Holiday Hearts Series
The Right Resolution[5]
The Cupid Caper[6]
Lucky in Love[7]
May I Have This Dance[8]
First Kiss Fireworks[9]
Falling For Her First Love[10]
Thankful for Love[11]
Mission: Mistletoe[12]
The Hearts and Hope Series
Shelter from the Storm[13]
The Doctor's Unexpected Family[14]

---

2. *https://books2read.com/LanguageOfLoveBook*

3. *https://books2read.com/LegacyOfLoveBook*

4. *https://books2read.com/LaborOfLove*

5. http://www.books2read.com/TheRightResolutionBook

6. http://www.books2read.com/TheCupidCaperBook

7. http://www.books2read.com/LuckyInLoveBook

8. http://www.books2read.com/MayIHaveThisDanceBook

9. http://www.books2read.com/FirstKissFireworksBook

10. https://books2read.com/FallingForHerFirstLoveBook

11. http://www.books2read.com/ThankfulForLoveBook

12. http://www.books2read.com/MissionMistletoeBook

13. http://www.books2read.com/ShelterFromTheStorm

14. http://www.books2read.com/TheDoctorsUnexpectedFamily

His Texas Princess[15]
Holiday of Hope[16]

Other Books by Kristen

Love Hallmark movies? Pick up Kristen's book October Kiss, based on the Hallmark movie viewers love! Available anywhere books are sold—in paperback, digital, and audio! October Kiss from Hallmark Publishing[17]

15. http://www.books2read.com/HisTexasPrincess

16. http://www.books2read.com/HolidayOfHope

17. https://www.books2read.com/OctoberKiss

About Kristen

KRISTEN ETHRIDGE WRITES Sweet Escape Romance—stories with hope, heart and happily-ever-after—for Harlequin's Love Inspired line, Hallmark Publishing, and Laurel Lock Publishing. She's a Romance Writers of America Golden Heart Award nominee and both a Christian Fiction and Inspirational Romance #1 Best-Selling Author.

You can find Kristen in her native habitat—a Texas patio—where she's likely to be savoring the joy of a crispy taco, along with a glass of iced tea. Scents from her essential oil diffuser are also a must, since she's a certified aromatherapist. She's almost convinced her family that it's normal to talk to imaginary people, as long it goes in a book.

Find her online at http://www.kristenethridge.com where you can get a free story for signing up for her newsletter. You can also follow her adventures in writing at www.facebook.com/kristenethridgebooks[1].

Keep up with Kristen by joining her newsletter list[2] and her author pages on Bookbub[3] and Facebook[4]. If you can't get enough of Port Provident, come join the Port Provident Community Center[5] on Facebook, the official gathering place for Kristen and her fans.

www.kristenethridge.com[6]

Facebook[7] Instagram[8]

The Port Provident Community[9] Center

Don't forget…if you love sweet escape romances, join Kristen's newsletter[10]!

---

1.   http://www.facebook.com/kristenethridgebooks

2.   http://www.kristenethridge.com/newsletter

3.   https://www.bookbub.com/authors/kristen-ethridge

4.   http://www.facebook.com/kristenethridgebooks

5.   https://www.facebook.com/groups/2422381554654795

6. http://www.kristenethridge.com

7. https://www.facebook.com/KristenEthridgeBooks

8. https://instagram.com/kristenethridge

9. https://www.facebook.com/groups/2422381554654795

10. http://www.kristenethridge.com

LAUREL LOCK PUBLISHING

Publisher's Note: This is a work of fiction. Names, characters, places, and incidents are a product of the author's imagination. Locales and public names are sometimes used for atmospheric purposes. Any resemblance to actual people, living or dead, or to businesses, companies, events, institutions, or locales is completely coincidental.

Scriptures taken from the Holy Bible, New International Version®, NIV®. Copyright © 1973, 1978, 1984, 2011 by Biblica, Inc.™ Used by permission of Zondervan. All rights reserved worldwide. www.zondervan.com[11] The "NIV" and "New International Version" are trademarks registered in the United States Patent and Trademark Office by Biblica, Inc.™

Book Layout ©2013 BookDesignTemplates.com

---

11.   http://www.zondervan.com/

www.ingramcontent.com/pod-product-compliance
Lightning Source LLC
Chambersburg PA
CBHW030353180626
46812CB00007B/2863